THE HUNTER

Book 2 of the Eternal Dominion Series

Levi Armstrong

Brave the Pall Publishing, LLC

Library of Congress Control Number: 9798991354325
Printed in the United States of America

To my band of brothers on B-Shift. It is an honor and a pleasure to serve alongside you all. May you never doubt the One who is with you in the fire. Always strive to be excellent. Stay safe!

CONTENTS

CONTENTS

PROLOGUE

It's been eight months since the world was nearly rewritten. After Id almost stole dominion and life as we know it all but spiraled into chaos, I asked myself for weeks, *"How do you ever come back from that?"* I saw the heavens open, and the justice of God immediately delivered! How could I ever resume a normal life after witnessing such things? I felt relentless, trenchant heat assail the wicked from on high! How could I ever doubt the Divine again?

I cried, "Hosanna!" And He answered me immediately...

Увы, I suppose I'm more like the Israelites than I once cared to admit. I witnessed profound miracles that should have burdened my soul so that I might be the most ardent follower, but still, I fail all the time. I still doubt. I still waste time on eternally irrelevant things. I'm still apathetic. Боже, измени меня!

No news sources apart from Huntsville's local media outlet made any mention of the atrocities that Lionel committed. The world carries on, unaware of the fact that oblivion was only moments away. Even what was reported from Huntsville was specifically related to the death of Jonathan, the two officers, and the fires that Id had caused. Nothing about what happened in the woods that night was told. Only we, the survivors know the truth. The spiritual consequence of what took place is lost to all but those who were there.

However, I fear that it is my duty to begin the next compilation of records, because despite its quaint setting amidst the rolling hills of northern Alabama, Allison has yet to harbor the summary of evils.

Included in this catalogue are accounts written by the Hunter himself that were only recently discovered.

- Grigory Yakor

CHAPTER 1

<u>The First Hunt</u>

In retrospect, I seldom thought about the creature that is most known as the Komodo dragon. Not only is his very appearance chilling, but his name itself demands respect, but what I appreciate most is the manner of the hunt. Komodo dragons are bold in their choosing of prey, and patient as they pursue it. Following their first contact with the victim, a Komodo dragon will continue to stalk its target for days with the most equanimous poise. He is in no rush, the toxic saliva that he introduced into the prey's blood stream will gradually kill off the vital organs and sooner or later, he will happily find his prey lying dead in some hovel that it thought would be safe from the long-abandoned enemy.

Fascinating, isn't it? I just had to try this artform! Albeit unorthodox, I was met with remarkable success following the choosing of my quarry. Duty tells me that I have no time to play around with prey. Indeed, there are much more efficient ways to accomplish my designs, but if I never stopped and savored the craft, I'd be a miserable wretch. My purpose endures, but I'm entrusted with just enough discretion in matters such as these.

†

A bold stag stood in the midst of his herd. None of them seemed too concerned with potential predators as they presumed confidence in their numbers. They appeared to thrive in the well-lit, lush, green clearing. I knew that to approach outright would spook the lot of them, and I'd lose my quarry.

Ah, but how do I employ my new method of blood-sport? How do I draw away the obvious leader of this rabble, so that I can exact the condemning strike?

He moved from the central mass of the herd and began exploring the grounds closer to the wood-line. He had yet to abandon the clearing, but he began branching out farther as his grazing continued. He seemed to find some sense of freedom as he stepped away from the herd. He all but avoided interacting with the other outlying deer as he rooted gently near a pine tree. What was his purpose in being so elusive, despite the herds obvious dependence on him? Some younger deer who weren't nearly as stout as he was watched his every move. A few seemed to be awaiting the chance to take his place as alpha, whilst others appeared to depend entirely on his every movement. Perhaps these were the behaviors that kept him on edge. That, and potential predators such as I.

The old stag progressed in my direction unawares. I silently crept to a well-covered brush. I knew that I would need to strike with inhuman speed if I was going to land a condemning blow. Also, I would have to close the distance rapidly. The faintest rustling of brush would be all that experienced stag required to make a hasty retreat. One snort, and the entire herd would scramble to action.

My fleshly disguise would seem innocuously familiar if the Stag didn't look too closely. Wearing this hide certainly has limitations, despite the thrill of intermingling so close to the prey.

However, I had to consider that when I delivered the toxin, my prize would almost certainly be alerted to my designs! Flight or fight would immediately ensue. I would have liked to think that —in the event of fighting— my fleshy frame might prove more useful than menial subterfuge. The confines of my disguise might very well be abandoned for the confirmation of the kill. However, my mask would no longer be of any use for future hunts if I did have to deliver an impromptu attack. Alas... an imperceptible strike was the only way to successfully complete the hunt.

With such resolve, I steadied myself and entered audible proximity. My movements were silent and unengaging. I approached indirectly and with seemingly arbitrary purpose. The proud stag observed my latest steps and glanced up only for a moment before concerning himself again with tasks befitting a creature of his station. He stepped close to a large oak tree, searching for something to graze upon. He no longer paid me any mind. Oh, the arrogance of these alpha males... he would soon aspirate on his own vanity!

I circumvented the base of the massive oak. Its girth was sufficient to muffle my leaf-crunching from the stag's ears and conceal my lurking from the eyes of the rest of the herd. The great beast's antlers scrubbed the scaly bark of my refuge. I slowed my breathing to minimize the pulse that I felt pumping at my temples like a drum. I drew a long, steady breath and poised. With a silent exhale, I lanced the animal's hide with the needling barb!

The muscular haunch twitched at the prick, but no other response was given. I remember the feeling of relief washing over me as the creature never looked in my direction but instead turned to face another more youthful stag who approached from the herd. I whipped back behind the tree before the encroaching deer could observe me. Thankfully, the barb's point was so acute that its piercing was unnoticed.

The two male deer returned to the herd together. I retreated to a concealed den of closely met trees. From that shade, I watched for a time with anticipation, but the poison's effect would be long-delayed, and like the dragon whom I so affectionately admire, I must pursue with meticulous restraint.

Marcus Spasmen's Catalogue of Clues to Invalidate the Supernatural: Entry #4, (June 19ᵗʰ, 2023)

It is noted here that the previous three entries are not included in this compilation due to their innocuous effect upon the mystery of the Hunter

A remote detonating device! That's how he did it!

I knew that the recurring payola to my privileged contact would, at last, reward me with substantial findings. After a handful of leads that only embittered my resolve, I've finally uncovered a quality clue!

Ever since the just execution of my former counselor, I have received dismissing remarks by Allison's finest whenever I bring up the necessity for more tangible evidence that would discredit the otherwise claimed supernatural characteristics of Lionel's crimes. In the eyes of Henry and his colleagues I may seem a bit eccentric, but they have already benefitted from my recordings. Even if they are not adorned with the spiritually poetic jargon that Henry soaked his narratives in. I'm sure it is not from religiosity that Henry's coworkers are content with his written contributions to the results of the "Id" case, but instead a slothful desire for an easy resolution.

My purpose, however, is not limited to the condemning of the late, wicked doctor, but also to silence the ludicrous notion of the presence of anything supernatural; particularly the works of "God".

If I ask anyone at the PD, they just tell me to "let it go." They've already got the guy, but I cannot simply abide their blind dismissiveness.

No! I must put the nail in the proverbial coffin.

Id was a man, and his deeds were done as a man. His downfall, too, was accomplished by men. Therefore, I must elucidate these truths to the masses of Allison and abroad.

As I was saying, I'm happy to record in the security of my journal that the further I have dug for answers, the more fruitful the discoveries have become!

The photos taken by APD's CSI unit after the church fire cause my heart to beat with greater rapidity as I continue to study them. Glimpses of symbols painted in broiled blood, a charred fireman's axe, eyebolts buried into the blackened church stage, and the ashen remains of a bear pelt captivate my senses as I am forced to relive what took place when FBC Allison all but burned to the ground with the Clemmenses and me inside. Amongst these snapshots of my second of four near death experiences in the past twelve months was a picture that has suddenly given new ardor to my quest!

A small black box with a screen no bigger than a calculator display was found behind the last row of charbroiled choir chairs upon the stage. It has some utterly melted mounting mechanism that must have been used to secure the device to the underside of any chosen surface. The detonator appeared to have two different ports at its top, but the plastic junctions and their internal wires melted away.

One of the ports must have been the extension of the antenna, whilst the other port was where the wires fed from the detonating device to the implanted explosives. Given the immediate billowing of flames, I wonder if he hadn't employed some lightweight, fuel-based explosive. Perhaps, he had filled the baptismal with gasoline, so he'd only need a miniscule explosion to initiate the fire. Thinking back, I don't recall smelling any petroleum fumes, but I was several... seven, I believe, rows back. Thus, I was well removed from the sniffing vicinity of the tank in which any of the local zealots were previously dunked.

If only I could find the transmitter that Lionel kept on his person that night! That discovery would be the quintessential evidence for my independent investigation. A finding like that might even shut Henry up about his "Divine Intercessor!"

Speaking of the heaven's supposed influence on Allison; the glen where Lionel was apprehended and the site that was described to be "laid bare" has vanished, or more appropriately, was never in place at all. For myself, I bear no recollection of that locale. The patch of forest (that simply looks like a sixty-foot gap between pines) where the blast theoretically took place has become a secluded spot to exchange money for information.

Ah, but my window of necessary labor is fast approaching. For the time being, I must endure the incessant lurking of Mrs. Antler over my shoulder, as I produce written works unlike anything this town has ever seen. The antiquated writing style of this newspaper, and its fixation on community events (which primarily pertain to church-goers, I might add), predictable weather patterns, and Mrs. Sherman's dainties is utterly repulsive. Incrementally, I must breach this grotesque mold.

Patience... I must have patience as I endure this trial. Progressive thought will be a slow integration for the paper, but I will nonetheless ensure its assimilation!

Following my shift today at the *Bale*, I am meeting my opportunistic contact at the "blast site" again, to exchange more substantial evidence. The quest for truth never rests, and I am her arbiter here in old, indigent Allison.

Letter from Henry Paul Loadwain to Misty Loadwain

My love, I'm at last keeping my promise to you.

I'm wild about you. I thought that I couldn't love you anymore than I did yesterday, but today I look at you anew. I see your curly brown hair fall over your shoulders, and I think again how incredible it is that you gave me a second thought. You look me in the eyes, not even with any real purpose in mind, just like, "Can you pass the peanut butter?", and I flush with warmth.

Even in routine interactions like these, I can't help thinking, with renewed appreciation, that I landed the catch of the century when you said, "Yes", and that every day since, I stay the most blessed guy in the world.

You're so patient when I'm not. You're so... thoughtful when I don't think quite enough about how my words may cut. And you're so forgiving, when I end up cutting you with my words.

I... I'm sorry. I don't ever want you to doubt my love. Sometimes my anger just rises so quickly, I don't even realize that it's there. I don't know. It could be my job. It could be my past. It could be the whole "Id" affair. Or... it could be that it's just in my personality to be a jerk, and the Lord is slowly grilling that out of me. Even if I fight the sanctifying process tooth-and-nail, both you and the Lord are so patient.

That's another thing... your faith is like the brick wall I need to lean against in my moments of weakness. And my weakness is shown a whole lot.

Honestly, I know that these past few months have been hard with losing the baby.

I think it's been bolstering for us both to be involved in the reconstruction of FBC Allison. Your organization of the church's legal documents and required permits, and all that stuff has made a world of difference for David and the other staff members. David and I were hanging the new sanctuary lights the other night, and he was telling me how much the church staff appreciated your administrative help. I told him that it pays to have the mayor's executive assistant for a wife!

What can I say? You excel in whatever area you put your mind to. You are faithful and diligent to the people you work with. Mayor Haldent has commented on multiple occasions of your stellar work ethic whenever Chief and I run over to town hall. I'm sure he can see the pride gleam from my face when I hear that. Without fail, my response is, "I definitely married up!"

I'm not trying to trick you with cheesy affection, or butter you up so that I can buy a boat, or something like that. I just don't want anything to happen, and I fail to tell you just how incredible you are. We aren't promised another minute. So right this second, may you know with certainty, that I adore you.

Private Journal of Grigory Yakor – 20 June 2023 (2322)

It's been an exceptionally long day, filled with a broad range of emotions. My twenty-four-hour shift concluded after twenty-five hours topped with a lengthy PCR for a deceased teenager.

It's always the same with suicides. They are found the following morning. The family and friends try to revive a blue corpse. We get there and we begin to move toward the resuscitation process. Oh, those moments are the worst, especially when obvious signs of death contraindicate any further treatment. Worse still is the loss of children.

This boy did not come from wealthy stock. He lived in not much more than a shack. His room was attached with pressboard and screws to the already flimsily constructed trailer. He was found by some adult female relative, of indetermined relationship. She cut him down, but it was far too late. She called, and we arrived in three minutes to the secluded trailer park. Everyone was standing on their porches at 0645, unabashedly gawking at us as we grabbed our resuscitative equipment and high-tailed it to the caller's address.

Lividity had set in. The blood pooled on the lower half of his body. The relative (aunt, maybe) had cut the cord from around his throat, but the deep indentation would remain there forever. Bulging eyes pled for another chance. Despite those globes being fogged over, they still showed instantaneous regret for his decision.

Only when they've crossed that last line, do they realize how wrong they were.

Every... single... time.

Rigor mortis caused the body to lay like a slim tree, with limbs bent in their last-ditch motions to rectify the error. There was nothing we could do.

He had been dead for hours.

What a miserable end to a shift. That wasn't the first to end like that, and it won't be the last.

The good news is that I was off from the ambulance. So, the day brightened emotionally in tandem with the sun's course! I spent the afternoon and evening with Lia. We drove first thing up into southern Tennessee and explored some quaint towns with historic markers. We even went and climbed onto a historic bridge. Lia didn't handle it well when I climbed up on the side railing, tottering over the canal.

When we got back in her car, I recommended getting samples at a nearby distillery that was offering tours, but she wasn't on-board with the idea, so we grabbed some coffee instead and found an antique bookstore along one of the downtown strips. She unearthed an old hardback copy of *Jude the Obscure*. I nodded to show respect, then smirked as I lofted my freshly discovered copy of *Crime and Punishment*.

She squinted, then read Dostoevsky's name and chuckled playfully with a shake of her head. Wait... Достоевский. Ah, that feels better.

Anyway, it was fun, scouring old bookshelves and learning more about each other's literary interests. She is partial to modern works, apart from some strange affection for anything written by Thomas Hardy. For her, romance was the MO, not the vivid, raunchy stuff, but the poetic and sappy ones *cue barfing*.

She also showed a keen interest in psychological thrillers.

I tried not to express my amusement too heavily, but thought to myself, "Spend enough time around people like me, and you'll find yourself in the midst of one."

Following our afternoon book-shopping, I took her to a nice restaurant in Winchester. Tonight, when I looked at her across the candle-lit dinner table, I knew —with perfect tranquility— that she was the one.

Sure, we've only been dating for a few months, but when you know... you know.

Somehow... I know.

We were just in the midst of discussing favorite seasons when my watch vibrated with a new page notification from the Fire-Alert app.

It read, "Medical Call – Critical – Possible 10-89 – PD Officer down."

The address was located in Bear Paw Creek. One of our wealthiest neighborhoods in Allison.

I was across the state line, so there was no reasonable way for me to do anything about it, but Henry's death flashed through my mind like a whip, and I apologized profusely to Lia before stepping outside to check on my dear friend.

I called twice. No answer.

Pacing the sidewalk, I wrestled for several moments deciding who to call next. C-Shift guys would still be on scene, so they couldn't answer. If Gamble was on scene, he wouldn't answer me, but somehow, I needed to know that Henry was ok.

Mark!

I scrolled through my contacts till I found a rather smug looking caller ID photo of "Marcus" peering philosophically at the camera. I was about to tap on the dial icon when a banner popped up, indicating a call from Henry.

Thank God, it was Henry's voice on the other line. Henry was safe.

Chief Isaac Knox, however, was not.

CHAPTER 2

No matter how much death I see, nothing shakes me like the glazed eyes of a friend.

Knox was so strong... so impervious. Nothing ever seemed to slow that man down. His work ethic was humbling. If I ever got to thinking that I was something special, I'd need only take one look over at Chief.

He was inhuman in his disciplines: both private and professional. He'd wake up at 0400 every day, even on weekends; read, weightlift, and then jog a couple miles on the treadmill before starting the day, which was usually very physically taxing in and of itself.

Knox didn't like excuses. I loved that quality about him... except for when I was the one who would try to excuse his mess-up. Then he would leave me speechless, because I knew he was right in calling me on my crap. There was no point in arguing with him. I didn't fear him, like some guys did. I loved him. I believed in him. He was the kind of leader that I want to be some day.

†

I met Jenny at the door. She showed up at Chief's house in her academy PT sweatpants and an *Eagles* t-shirt that looked to have been bought at one of their debut concerts, given the faded color, worn logo, and the pinholes along the seam. Her hair was tied back in a half-considered ponytail.

As I approached, she turned to me with wide-eyes and heavy breathing. The disbelief was waylaying us both. Together, we went in to see him.

The room was stuffy and uncomfortably still. EMS had just stepped out after recording the absence of any heart-rhythm. A thin white sheet lay over a perfectly still body atop the bed.

Jenny and I approached the corpse without uttering a word. She reached a hand to lift the sheet but pulled it back before touching him. I heard her breath catch as she turned away and walked out of the room. Taking one last step forward, I unveiled what Jenny could not.

Knox was pale, with eyes closed. His skin stiff and cold, in the all-too-familiar rigidity of death. He passed in his sleep.

I said to myself, "He's only fifty-nine... was fifty-nine," I then added with sorrowful correction.

I began examining the room after laying the sheet back over the man who bore such dignity, even in death.

His nightstand upheld a black and copper colored alarm clock with a radio dial built in, a small reading lamp, bi-fold picture frame of Karen and Lucas when they were teenagers, a bottle of pills, and a half-empty glass of water.

I knelt to study the pills without touching them.

A familiar voice entered the room behind me.

"It's his blood pressure medicine." Gary interpreted the technical drug name for me.

I trust Gary's twenty-six years of experience on the ambulance, so I stood and turned to him, dumping some of my shock on him, hoping he'd make sense of it.

"What happened?" I asked with an exasperated breath; finally starting to acknowledge that Chief was really gone.

"We can't know for certain until the coroner examines him, but honestly, Henry, it looks like sudden cardiac arrest. Happened in the best way too: asleep, at home, and in bed."

Suddenly, a wail cut through the air, from the other side of the house. Over Gary's shoulder, Jenny jumped out of her skin and whipped her head around.

I leaned around Gary's other shoulder to see where that noise came from. I began to process simultaneously Gary's unsurprised reaction and a faint familiarity in the voice that brought about the scream. The voice that I recognized was that of Mrs. Carolyn Knox. Evidently, she was awoken by some strange gut feeling. Without any word or sign, she knew something was wrong with Isaac.

Reportedly, Carolyn woke from deep sleep, already knowing that Isaac was gone.

It just continues to blow my mind that someone so strong, so healthy could die of sudden cardiac arrest, at a relatively early age, with no warning signs.

It's just... somehow wrong. I know everything happens for a purpose, a piece of God's divine plan, but some parts of the plan are just so hard to reason with.

I returned to the living room and found Carolyn on the sofa being consoled by a younger female EMT who I didn't recognize.

Kneeling beside Mrs. Knox, I embraced her in an affectionate, one-shouldered hug. I half expected her to push me away, but she buried her face into my other shoulder and began wailing again. I held on to her and felt my throat catch sharply, and watering in my eye.

Not now! I commanded from my thoughts; *She needs you.*

Glancing up at a sniffing, red-eyed Jenny, and a stunned Gamble who had just hastily stopped in the doorway, I silently lowered my head onto Carolyn's petite shoulder and demanded even more of myself.

They all need you.

Marcus Spasmen's Personal Memoirs (June 21st, 2023)

Henry was in depressing sorts when I arrived at his house this morning. Misty led me onto the back porch of the home, where an existential detective sat, philosophizing over a coffee cup that had long gone cold. He mindlessly spun the mug around with his finger on the hand loop.

I coughed, having already heard the dreadful news, I didn't want to intrude his emotional processing.

I read about graduated grieving theory in one of my psychology textbooks from college. This was that exact occurrence, given the nature of what he had just experienced. He observed first-hand the loss of a long-time friend, mentor, and leader. The acute emotional stress only compounded with the consideration of other recent... losses.

All that being said, Henry certainly benefitted from my psychological/counseling studies. I knew just the thing to say, and what not to say as he sought to bounce back from his miserable night.

"Wouldn't you say that the healthiest thing we can do is find another mystery to solve, ole' boy?"

He did not respond, so I added lightheartedly,

"Something to relocate your already troubled mind."

Henry graced me with a sedate chuckle, then followed up with a question that gave me all the permission I needed.

"And, what kind of mystery do we need to uncover?" He asked with the faintest twinge of curiosity.

With a brotherly slap on the shoulder, I walked around to the other side of the patio table and sat in the seat juxtaposed to him.

"How's work?"

He shot an ambivalent glance. I immediately corrected my careless inquiry.

"I mean, apart from the disheartening loss of your Chief; have you any new and thrilling cases to report? I, for one, found the case of the cauterized squirrels very engaging."

Again, Henry's hard gaze told me that I should stop talking.

I didn't consider that the case of a pubescent criminal who sadistically cut apart and burned little woodland creatures for fun was really too sensitive of a topic to bring up. Really, as cases go, it wasn't overly exciting; just morbid.

However, I will say that from a psychological perspective, the juvenile —who now resides in Wilkins Detention and Reformatory— would serve as an engrossing case-study for any student of the mind.

After one mandatory meeting with the onsite chaplain, that troubled youth began touting his innocence and confessing that he had been possessed by a demon. It was a futile attempt, on my part, trying to convince him otherwise. By the incessant rumors about Id, coupled with that sycophant chaplain filling the boy's head with metaphysical rubbish, the youth was bound to placate upon the age-old ploy of spiritual influences.

The breadth of my internal digression afforded Henry some indeterminate moments of silence, until I broke it with a much more pointed question.

"Does anything about this feel odd to you?"

A third glance from Henry bore a distinctly different emotion. No longer was he annoyed at my —perhaps ill-timed — comments. Instead, his reddened eyes looked at me with longing. His pain was laid bare, and he didn't care to cover it up anymore.

Without any verbal input, I knew that he wanted... No, he needed an explanation for Chief Knox's death. Something more realistic than the most in-shape man in Allison keeling over dead from "natural causes".

Interpreting his expression in the affirmative, I began to speculate aloud.

"I mean, was he doing anything overly strenuous the day prior?" I asked.

"He was at the PD with me, most of the day." Henry replied.

"But, y'all were just doing deskwork, office stuff, etc.?"

Henry snorted through his nostrils in disbelief. Apparently, I was being condescending, somehow.

"Yeah, he made it to his office early, as always. We spoke briefly about his tendonitis that had flared up in his right elbow. We spoke about the men's meeting at church next Sunday, and about upcoming reassignments to new vehicles. The city finally saw fit to invest in three new patrol cars."

"What? No more Crown Vic?" I chided gently. "Do you even know how to operate a car made after the year 2000?"

"Ha-ha" Henry admitted. "I suppose that I'll have to figure it out quickly."

A smirk rested on Henry's face as he forgot the darkness of the day for but a brief moment.

"If you don't mind me asking, Henry, who could have held a grudge against Knox? I mean, anyone who stands out in your mind out of the hundreds, if not thousands of... no probably just hundreds of criminals that Knox put behind bars. Anyone who would have access to him, and who would benefit from his death?"

"Mark, I do appreciate what you're trying to do here. Raise suspicion and spur me on into another case. There is a part of me that wishes it were what you suppose, so I could hunt down the crook and bring him to justice for killing a good man." He said that through gritted teeth.

After a moment's pause, he continued in a softer voice, "It's not's so easy of an explanation, this time. Sometimes, good people just die unexpectedly and for no reason at all."

His words faltered at the last.

I had nothing more to say. I silently stood up, walked by him and his motionless, cold cup of coffee. Before I reached the back door of the house I stopped and turned half-way around. Placing a hand on my friend's shoulder, I gave it a gentle squeeze and looked out upon his peaceful back yard, with the ever-babbling brook and the distant wood-line.

It was there that my attention was arrested, and I thought I saw Gamble. Amidst the pines, past the edge of Henry's property, I saw Gamble raise his hand to his ear. Immediately my phone started vibrating in my pocket.

"I'm so sorry, Henry. Call me whenever you have the time."

At that, I spun round and went through the house, with a kindly wave and a "thank you" to Misty before returning to my car.

I had missed the call, but pulling out onto County Rd. 53, the returned call was answered by Gamble.

"Mark"

"Yeah, what's up?"

"I think I found something in the woods. Are you still at Henry's?"

"And how exactly did you know I was at Henry's?"

"Because I saw you just a minute ago."

"And what are you doing skulking out in the woods behind his house?"

"Just drive around to our usual meeting spot. When you get there, keep walking past the marked tree by about fifty yards then step through the dense brush to your right."

"Are you going to meet me there, or just keep traipsing Henry's land?"

"Just hurry up, man!"

†

I managed to duck and wriggle my way through the dense foliage to arrive at the spot that Gamble indicated. Climbing to my feet, I stopped and gaped with a slack jaw.

After rubbing my eyes twice and pinching myself once, I accepted the reality of a large clearing with dozens of felled and disintegrating pine trees. This spot, I of course recognized. It was what lay at the epicenter from which all the trees had collapsed that caused me to swear with incredulity. A large crater, which was not there before, now yawned in the middle of the woodland realm.

I couldn't resist the wonder of it all. Mindless, I approached the crater and marveled for several moments at its size. Its depth and breadth were surely not overlooked on my previous visits to the glen. I was overcome with a very strange sensation, the longer I stared at the cavity, the more I knew that I recognized the new additions to the spot. It all felt so… abstruse.

I know that isn't much of a rational annotation, but it was a very surreal experience that I have yet to fully come to grips with.

Along the side and base of the earthen bowl, was a prolific interweaving of morning-glories. The vined flowers were open wide in a posture of reception. They basked, soaking in every ounce of sunlight.

My curiosity expanded as I considered that it was almost sunset and I was under a canopy of trees. These flowers are usually closed by this time of day, and presumably should be, given the poor lighting. Looking directly above me, my inquisitiveness climaxed as one clearly definable circle remained cut amongst the branches of the trees. It was an unhindered window to the orange evening sky above.

I blinked numerous times, peering at these most-efficient morning glories, until my peripherals caught sight of some upturned dirt just to the left of the crater.

It appeared to have been where something was buried then withdrawn from the soil. Some object that was thin in form, but long enough to have sunk into the tightly packed dirt. Whatever it was, it left a lean slot of hardened dirt. The perimeter of the slot was black, but soil everywhere else was brown. Something had solidified the hole, presumably with heat.

"The question is, 'How recent—'"

My thought was cut off by Gamble's call.

"Mark, there you are! Come check this out!" He began walking toward the far side of the clearing.

"Wait!" I demanded. "You knew about this crater?"

"No, I found it today. That's part of why I called you so quickly. We both have been trying to disprove that this site ever existed. Until today, we had done a damn good job."

Flabbergasted, I responded, "Bu- wha?? What do you mean? This can't be the same place that Henry wrote about!"

I took another sweep around the clearing with my saucer-eyes. At last, looking back at Gamble, "Can it?" I whimpered.

"I know, it's not in the same spot as Henry described, but what about that?" Gamble gesticulated excitedly, pointing to the crater.

"But we can talk more about that later! You've got to see this!" He hurriedly retraced his steps to the far side.

"What do you mean 'not in the same spot?'" I mumbled.

I staggered after him, with a mind that raced like a hamster on a wheel. Except the hamster lost control and was spun round and round.

Gamble held back the branches so I could step through. When I passed by and looked ahead, I fell into a sort of stupor. I couldn't speak for several moments as my subconscious orientation was tossed into a blender and set on high. I think I tilted my head, like they do in the movies. As if the movement would afford me clearer comprehension.

At last, the hamster was sent barreling into the wall of the cage. What sent me into pure befuddlement was the sound of the babbling brook and the sight of Henry's back-porch in the distance!

I couldn't openly admit that I remembered where the "Site of Dominion" (as my religious cohorts called it) was, because when I previously went looking for it, I found nothing to do with a beam of light or a hole in the ground. Now, however, I couldn't escape the site's existence!

We had been meeting in this glen with the felled trees, but it didn't have that bizarre crater, the divine skylight, those persistent morning glories, or even that curious charred hole. I don't understand how I arrived at this quagmire by taking the same route that once led to our normal meeting place. It's the exact same path, but now the end result is different! Indeed, what made matters worse, and what berated my mind was the conflict between where I deep down once knew it to be, and where I was finding it now. Henry's house is on the west end of town, which is nowhere near where Gamble and I had been meeting. Where we formerly met near Adam's house was on the east end of town, and County Rd. 53 divides the woods behind the two residences.

"It... It..."

I dared not say the words out loud. Even writing it now feels like a means of offering myself up to insanity.

Damn it all! Things would have been so much simpler if this place had just stayed absent! What am I to do now with this discovery??

charcoal shade of black moving about in the gloom of the night. At last, I was resolved that he had finally gone and that I could breathe again.

A moaning cry came from upstairs, it sounded like it came from Merrin's room. I was up the stairs in the blink of an eye, and I burst through Merrin's door. She was tossing and turning as I approached her bed.

"Hey baby-doll. You ok?"

She continued to squirm in her bed. She wasn't saying anything, just breathing as though something in her dreams was making her anxious. I went to turn her bedside lamp on, but when I twisted the dial, we remained in darkness. However, as soon as the dial had clicked, I saw that Merrin stopped squirming.

"Baby?" I asked the small shadow that laid perfectly still.

Before I could react, the little figure sat up and gave a deafening scream so that my mind nearly went into a panic!

Instinctively, I hugged her. Clutching her safely in my embrace, the scream soon died off, and her frantic breathing slowed. After a moment, the room was quiet again, and Merrin once again let out a petite modicum of a snore. I kept holding her, ensuring that she was truly asleep, and those lingering seconds gave my older, less adaptable heart time to start to slow.

Eventually, I laid her back down onto her pillow and pulled the blanket up to her chin. It was just when I leaned forward to kiss her forehead that I heard that metal against metal screeching from the front door. Without even stopping to think, I stood up from her bed and made my way to the staircase.

My heart, again, beat like the hoofs of a race-horse. I began to hear that same tense voice speaking into my house,

"Do you mind if I come in?"

Upon recognizing the sound, I began skipping steps and

jumping to the halfway landing.

"Uh, sure." Owen's innocent little voice spoke.

I leapt all the way down the last flight and crashed to the ground. I stumbled forward into the hallway and turned to my left to see Owen standing at the half open door.

"Owen!" I cried. The darkness of the night outside seemed to almost press in through the doorway.

Fists clenched; I ran to the door to throttle the man who just spoke to my son. Just as I reached for the doorknob to open it wide, the door slammed shut with a crash that shook a nearby picture off the wall. I grabbed Owen and pulled him toward me.

"What in the world is going on, Adam?" Kelly called from the door of our bedroom. "Owen? Why are you out of bed, young man?"

"Where is he?" I asked, gripping the boy's shoulders and failing to keep my voice from cracking.

"Who?"

"What do you mean 'who'? The man who just asked if he could come in."

I heard Kelly gasp as I uttered the words.

"I... I don't know."

"Kelly, shotgun."

She returned to the bedroom and came back a moment later with my 12-gauge. I searched through the house while Kelly continued to caress her baby boy and soothe her own anxiety.

My search completed in every room, I returned to the hallway near the front door and appeased Kelly, explaining that no one else was in the house, still not entirely convinced myself.

I escorted Owen with a shotgun in hand back to his bedroom. I checked his closet and under his bed one more time before laying him down. He seemed unfazed by all that went on. After kissing him on the forehead and tucking him in, I went back to the hallway, where Kelly stood, this time with her own handgun at the ready. I let out a half-hearted chuckle as I approached her. She was crying.

"I can't go through that again, Adam. Not again!"

My heart pounded in my chest as I thought back on all the horrors we faced last fall.

"We won't." I assured her with a hug. Yet, I struggled to believe my own words.

My God, I pray that we won't.

The Second Hunt

I've spent a lot of time trapping foxes. The key to seamless trapping is subtlety. The fox doesn't need to know that anything has changed in its environment. Simply slide the treadplate underneath the most frequently traipsed path. Let death lay open beneath their feet. No need to coax the animal to pursue some suspicious allurement. He trusts what he knows. Let the fox think that he knows every step he takes. The musings of the mind keep attention best when the environment is most familiar. Hide in normalcy so that the creature will not even perceive you in broad daylight.

My prey rose early, as was calculated. He went about his mindless routine, as the doomed creature stepped into the hovel where I knew he would plan to spend the next several hours. His safe place was perceivably undisturbed. However, the beast would soon find that I had been in position, awaiting his arrival.

The animal skirted through the dark opening. There was no hesitation, despite being blind. At the rate of his advance, I silently took a sharp breath of anticipation.

Any moment no-

My thought was interrupted by the damning crash.

The trap sprung flawlessly! My mortal frame quivered with ecstasy as the harsh clang of a closing mechanism was melodiously met with the cracking of bones.

Mmm... I can still smell the blood that spurted across my face as his legs gave way to chomping steel.

The poor creature never made a sound. That might be the most interesting facet of the hunt. No squeal, no moan, no cry. This occurrence is not unheard of, however. Throughout the years, I've slain beasts that failed to bewail their termination.

I've come to understand it as some deficit of the brain. Distinct types of trauma could cause a maladaptive response in the face of death. Self-preservation is nowhere to be found. These impaired creatures do not react at all to the immediate threat. Instead of crying out, running, or fighting, the animal falls; passively assuming its fate.

I approached the maimed and bleeding fox. He writhed back and forth unconsciously, but the only sounds I heard were gasps of pain. The agony must have been deeply consuming, because it took some time for it to notice my approach from the shadows. A shimmer of twilight sliced through the den, affording me a glimpse of his face. Bewildered eyes expanded when he finally acknowledged me.

His breathing audibly accelerated.

I usually would have unceremoniously flicked my knife across his throat, killing with dutiful efficiency. At that moment, however, something gave me pause. I knew that there was still much to do, but I took this momentary delay to examine my prey more closely.

Amidst fidgets and gasps, he raised a leg to try to reposition and catch an unhindered breath. I put my foot down and cracked another leg.

At last, I evoked a whimper!

What was it about this fox that intrigued me so?

I gripped one of the two uninjured limbs and cranked it to the side, exposing what I suspected that I would find. The mark on his breast told me what breed this wretch was. That confirmation married my duty with delight.

I then deemed it fitting to spare a few minutes.

I took my broiling knife and made the vile creature wail till there was no breath left in his lungs!

<u>Private Journal of Grigory Yakor – 22 June 2023 (0900)</u>

I got back to my house this morning, unsure of what to do. Lia was already at the hospital, eleven hours left in her twelve-hour shift, and I'm off from the ambulance today. I need to go to the gym, but I've had trouble focusing on anything since yesterday. So much… so fast.

My eyes flashed to the liquor cabinet. Then, my gaze shifted to the humidor box, where my pipe and tobacco lay. I took two steps toward the kitchen, unconsciously gliding the counter with my hand. Before I reached the cabinet, my hand ran upon a familiar texture. I stopped.

Looking down, my hand was resting on my Bible. I looked up at my bottle of vodka, then at the humidor before turning back to the only real solution to the tumult in my mind.

It felt like I'd been holding my breath for hours. It was as if I had been hypoxic since that last call yesterday. Surveying my yard from the back porch, I sat down in my "old man rocking chair" (as Lia calls it). I thumbed the pages of the Psalms. I knew that King David was acquainted with suffering and violence, but he was still able to find peace.

"Peace; that's exactly what I don't have," I thought aloud.

I trembled as I began to read.

"Hear my cry, O God, listen to my prayer;"

Fire churned behind my eyes, when I anxiously closed them.

"From the end of the earth I call to You when my heart is faint."

Cody's scream pierced my ears repeatedly.

"Lead me to the Rock that is higher than I,"

That dread of being unable to save my friend caused my heart to thump heavily in my chest.

"For You have been my Refuge,"

A woman's straining cry racked my head, and I shook uncontrollably.

"A strong tower against the enemy."

The crushed father, and the lifeless child... mercilessly mangled.

"Let me dwell—"

"Oh God, how? How could such things be? How could You allow this to happen? It's one thing to say that You are just, and You are right in all that You do; believing that when You take a life, it is part of Your good sovereignty. But, to see lives taken like this... I... I am tormented. I trust... no, I know that You are good. But this pain, this loss... it is... it doesn't feel good." I prayed aloud without any regard for who else might be hearing. I needed to speak my vulnerability aloud, otherwise the haunts in my mind would have consumed me.

My eyes returned to the text, clinging to the Light.

"Let me dwell in Your tent forever."

Then, I thought of the man now dwelling in God's tent forever.

"Let me take refuge under the shelter of your wings! Selah."

At the command to pause and reflect, I wept bitterly. I don't remember what I said next, but there, on my porch, I was slumped forward, heaving tears and whispering passionately to the Lord about my fears, my pains and the unbearable loss that those families are feeling now.

I can't recount all the words I spoke to Him, but through some imperceptible exchange, that time on the porch became one of the warmest, most tender moments of my life. Somehow, I was assured in the midst of my mental and emotional torment, the King of Heaven, the Commander of life and eternity, embraced me, hiding me in the shelter of His wings.

I grieve the boy. I grieve his father, and I grieve the mother who saw them die. Also, I grieve my Sunday School teacher. I will live my life; honoring their memory. May I never forget the pain of their loss. Oh God, keep apathy at bay, and cause me to feel the weight of every life I meet.

Private Journal of Grigory Yakor – 22 June 2023 (1600)

I don't typically write in my journal twice in one day, but I feel that I am now ready to face more fully what I wrestled with earlier. I called Lia on her lunch break and we talked a little bit. I didn't get too specific with her but shared enough to communicate the gist of what happened.

I think it best to address now, and in extensive detail, the major events of the past thirty-six hours.

†

I got to the station at 0640, per normal. I was in the parking lot, about to open my bible and I heard the tones ringing inside the station. I looked at the alert page on my phone and saw "flames visible." Reading the address, I whipped my head to the east and saw the confirmation surging in an ever-heightening black plume!

I hopped out of my truck and ran inside. Bumping into A-shift as they were running for the bay door, I slipped by and grabbed my bunker gear. I just happened to glance down and see a text from Cody, on my watch as I was throwing my gear in the truck.

"Grab my gear. I'll meet you there!"

In a split-second decision, I gathered up his helmet, pants, boots, coat, mask and radio. The truck was pulling out before I even shut the cab door. The address was only a mile away, so I was frantically flinging my gear on.

Thankfully, automaticity took over, and I was donned and "armor-tight, ready-to-fight" in about forty seconds. We rolled up on scene to a single story, brick structure with flames billowing out two windows nearest the garage on the bravo side. The residents were in the neighbor's yard across the street. They confirmed that everyone was out of the house.

Willard pulled the line, and I helped him stretch and flake it out. Terry had the truck in pumping gear only moments before the line was laid out and ready to go. We put our masks on, checked each-other's quickly before giving Terry the signal. The line was charged, Willard bled the line of any air by cracking the nozzle open, then he shut it back and we made entry into the garage door, leading into the house.

Black smoke filled the top two-thirds of the hall. We advanced low and fast. The ambient heat was quickly detectable as we approached the other end of the hall. Willard turned the corner as I pulled extra slack right behind him. We were hit with a wall of flame where the kitchen should have been.

"Get after it, son!" I cheered Willard on, as he opened the nozzle and began to put water on the fire.

Our vision blurred as steam, smoke and black chunks of debris overcame us.

Willard kept knocking back the wall of heat. As soon as there was a noticeable recession in the orange glow, I spurred Willard on to advance. We pushed our way into the kitchen and extinguished the last of the flames.

With the windows already blown out, the smoke and steam began to clear within a minute. After searching around the kitchen, adjoining dining and living rooms, I gave the favorable radio report.

"Interior to Command: fire is out at this time!"

I let out a whoop and patted Willard on the back. Our bottles still had about 2700 psi remaining, so we stood up and began to walk around, searching for remaining pockets of fire.

I took the New York hook and began tearing down some ceiling. Willard shot into the openings and we drained our air bottles in this manner. Leaving the hose on the ground, we opened the front door, which was across the far end of the dining room and exited the house. We met Cody and Captain Andrews just outside. They helped us take our packs off and set them down on the rehab tarp that had been laid out.

"Did ya save me any?" Cody asked with an admiring smirk.

"Eh... Maybe an ember or two." I responded with a satisfied exhale and wink.

"Well, Cap and I are gonna keep overhauling. Y'all drink some water and rehab for a couple minutes. We'll be right back." Cody gave me a pat on the shoulder before moving inside.

Willard handed me an ice-cold water bottle from the cooler.

"You're the man, Willard! You should switch to B-Shift."

"Haha, maybe **you** should join us on A-Shift. As you saw, we get the job done!"

"I can't argue wit—"

My response was cut off by a loud crash and wail from inside the house.

"Блин!" I shot to my feet. "Cody! Cap!"

Everyone who had been out on the fireground ran for the door. Willard and I were inside first and found a large section of smoldering roofing heaped on the floor, covering the breadth of the kitchen. I scanned the room for my brothers, when Cody's PASS device began to beep from underneath the pile of rubble!

We converged on the pile like magnets and tore away charred timbers, ceiling plaster, and ductwork. Cap emerged from the rubble and was pulling an unresponsive Cody out with him! We immediately carried him out of the house and began treating him in the yard.

With cervical spine considerations, we performed a rapid trauma assessment. No DCAP-BTLS. The only alarming findings were the unresponsiveness and the mechanism of injury. I hopped in the back of the ambulance and began helping with Cody's care.

We assessed his vital signs. His airway was patent, his breathing was regular, and his pulse was strong and slow. I could feel my own heartbeat slow, as I started to realize that he was momentarily stable. Regardless, he was struck hard enough to go unconscious, and that was cause for concern. I gave Cody a sternal rub and shouted his name. There was no response. I rifled through the ambulance cabinet and found an ammonia capsule. Cracking it, I waved it repeatedly right below Cody's nostrils. He winced and turned his head away, but didn't open his eyes. He started to moan for a moment, then stopped.

The monitor indicated a significant drop in his blood pressure and his heart rate. Gary started an IV line with a fluid bolus, and within minutes had brought Cody's systolic up to 90mmHg.

I assisted JCEMS with their patient until Gary gave me a head nod, indicating that it was time for them to roll out. Hesitatingly, I backed out of the rear doors of the ambulance. Looking one more time at my firefighter brother; disbelieving that he was actually lying there, unconscious, pale as death, and sweaty as a Siberian in the South.

The ambulance door slammed shut in my face, and the sirens began to howl as the truck pelted me with gravel in its departure. I stood there for a moment. Then I buried those thoughts in a box in my mind and returned to the work of salvage and overhaul.

Captain Andrews was being tended to by a second ambulance crew of younger EMT's that I didn't recognize. As I returned to the house with my head down, I saw in my periphery that Cap was watching me closely. Inattentive to the hands that cared for his wounds, I felt his gaze, adamantly fixed on me. I thought nothing of it at the time. Now, I can't help but reason that he blames me for not more effectively extinguishing the flames in the attic space. Worse still, I know he's right. I must have missed something.

I haven't even gone to see Cody yet. I don't think he'd want me there. How can I go visit his sickbed, knowing that it's my negligence that nearly killed him?

†

This could be an illusion that I've adopted, but usually, it feels as though after a house fire, you've sort of... "earned the day". It's probably the way I perceive it because of the irregularity in which we come upon actual working structure fires in Allison. If one of my children is reading this and happens to be working at a large city department, they are scoffing at me right about now.

All that being said, my presumption about earning the day was brutally disproved yesterday.

Willard got held over to work with us on B-Shift, since Cody was staying in the hospital. We had just finished scrubbing the hoses and rinsing off our air packs when a Signal 8: "wreck with injuries" came over the radio. Dispatch added to the report, "T-Boned; possible entrapment".

We dropped our brushes and buckets. I slung my wet pack into the seat bracket and donned my bunker gear. We were sailing down the road again, blaring sirens and flashing lights to the second of three tragedies for that day.

†

Arriving on scene, we saw a black pickup with a decimated bumper and crumpled hood. Pieces of plastic headlights were scattered everywhere. The driver of the truck was stumbling about, swearing aloud, and imploring for the health of the people in the other car.

At the other car, three or four people were huddled. Those closest to driver's side door were shouting incoherently and shaking their heads. One person was at the passenger window, tending to that occupant. We yelled for the crowd to step back. And when they did...

I will never forget what I saw.

What was I to do? There... There was nothing I could do. The driver was crushed between his door that intruded all the way to the center console. He had been killed instantly. I looked across and saw that the female passenger in the front had an angulated fracture of her left humerus, a large contusion on the left side of her skull, visibly labored breathing. A bystander -a heavy set, middle-aged woman with greasy, brown hair- was holding C-Spine stabilization. I communicated with the patient and the bystander that I was coming around and we were going to get her taken care of. She didn't seem to hear me. I immediately stood up and took a step back.

That was the moment when I finally acknowledged the rear passenger on the driver's side.

Боже мой! Я не могу...

The remains of a child who also had been struck directly by the pickup were... everywhere.

{Prepare yourself, my children. I pray you never have to see the unbridled ugliness of the world, but if you do, be sure to share your pain with those you trust, otherwise it will consume you. Forgive me for sharing mine with you}

I was frozen in horror.

Then, the greasy-haired woman shouted to get my attention. Into the invisible box, went any feelings about the child.

I ran around to the other side of the car. The bystander maintained hold of the C-Spine while I did a rapid trauma assessment. The occupant was unresponsive but breathing. I was able to palpate a carotid pulse. Her skin was ashen and sweaty. She was deteriorating rapidly. We needed to move her right away. Willard came up with the short spine board and a c-collar. He began speaking to the patient, explaining what he was about to do in securing the collar around her neck.

Surprisingly, she started to move and speak incoherently.

The greasy- haired woman stepped back before Willard had his hands on the patient's head. In that momentary span of semi-cognizance and range of motion, she turned and witnessed true horror.

The first sound she made was a sharp sucking in of her lower lip, as she gasped to see what was left of her husband.

"N—n—no, no, no." The no's got louder the longer she looked.

Willard tried to calm her and get her to follow commands, but she didn't give him any attention.

"Ma'am," Willard tried again, but it was at this point that she woke up fully and her deepest instinct was aroused. She gasped again as she turned her head further back to what was behind her husband.

"Ох, Боже, помилуй!"

There will never be a more horrifying sound in my life. The cry of that mother will haunt me for the rest of my life. All of us froze. Despite her own life being in jeopardy, we couldn't help but be stunned by the awful wail of a mother who lost everything she treasured in one grotesque moment. The scream lasted several agonizing moments, but when it finally fell off, her eyes rolled back in her head, and I told Willard to hold her head steady so it wouldn't drop forward.

We put the c-collar around her neck, then moved her out of the vehicle with the short spine board. Thankfully, we first tried the passenger door handle before getting the hydraulic cutters out. We quickly loaded her into the back of the ambulance and shut the door. Removing her outer garments, we were finally able to get a clear picture of her injuries.

She did have a flail segment in her ribs, presenting with paradoxical motion and ecchymosis along her left axillary region. Her left arm was bent as if she had two elbows. The direct impact of the console against her arm caused a mid-humeral fracture. The left side of her forehead presented with a steadily growing hematoma. I hooked her up to the monitor, so that we could get a clear set of baseline vitals.

Gary, who had just got back in town from dropping Cody off at the hospital was now starting an IV in the patient's right antecubital fossa. Her blood pressure was 64/36, O2 saturation was 87%, pulse was 40 beats per minute, and her respirations were slow and irregular.

I tore open the supply cabinet closest to the captain's seat and dug out a CPAP device. Hooking the device up to the ambulance's oxygen port, I began continuous positive air pressure to help provide a constant supply of oxygenated air and prevent any further collapse of the flail segment with undue weight upon the lungs. Over the next few minutes, the paradoxical motion decreased and her oxygen saturation rose. While observing the respiratory improvement, I looked again at the darker area of bruising toward the lower portion of where the axillary ribs had been struck. I communicated that finding to Gary, who nodded and said, "She's probably got a splenic rupture. Thanks for the help, it's time to go!"

I stepped out and shut those double doors for the second time that day. Again, I was pelted with gravel as tires spun, and lights and sirens announced the procession of another critical patient bound for Huntsville.

Jenny from CSI came and took several photos of the bodies and the wreckage. The plunks of empty beer cans jangled across the morosely still scene, as Jenny opened the passenger door. Everyone turned to look at the truck driver, who was being tended to for his minor injuries. The younger EMT who was with the driver, turned and gave a look to Jenny and me. Flaring her nostrils, and pointing to her nose, we interpreted her message. Jenny turned away from the wind and spoke into her radio.

One of the two cops who were directing traffic hopped in his patrol car and pulled up right next to the truck. Within two minutes, three other cop cars appeared, as if they had been waiting in the tall grass for this precise moment. I looked for my dear friend Henry, but he was not there. Nor was Gamble. Jenny shook her head sorrowfully and resumed her macabre photography as the inebriated driver was forcefully stuffed into the back of the cop car.

Following Jenny's evidence gathering and the unforgettably disquieting task of extricating the bodies from the vehicle, we awaited the wrecker company to remove both the car and the truck from the roadway.

"Damn" is all Cap said with an air of disbelief when we got back in the truck, headed to the station. I didn't say it, but I agreed. It was the worst day on record, in my mind. After restocking supplies and filling out reports, I attempted a workout while I was already sweaty and filthy from the day's trials, but my motivation and energy were lacking.

After benching far below my max, and a depressing display of an abdominal workout, I drank some protein and took a shower. It was high time that I washed the grime of that day off me.

After getting clean, I sat down to reheat my leftovers and have an early supper. Cap had already eaten without us. Willard planned to order some fast food to be delivered, but he was too busy doomscrolling through fishing and hunting videos on his phone. I stopped to pray before eating and took a deep breath, burying my hands in my face. With my eyes closed, I was in a posture of prayer, but my mind raced. After several moments of failing to commune with the Father I began to eat.

Following supper, I grabbed *Crime and Punishment* and sat in the recliner. I thumbed my way to the moment of Raskolnikov's fell deeds when Willard walked in with his to-go bag of fast food.

I then thought it would be good to spend a little time hanging out together. It might have bettered our spirits.

"You want to find a movie to watch?" I asked.

"Sure," Willard responded with his slow and heavy, country boy accent. "What you wanting to watch?"

"You know, I've been really curious about the new—"

My thought was cut off by the tones resounding throughout the station.

"Attention Allison Fire, attention Allison Fire, possible 10-89 from assault. Location: Simm's Drugs. Stage until scene is secure."

Willard and I looked at each wide-eyed, as we made our way down the hall to the bay.

"What the Hell is going on today?" Willard cried aloud as he slammed the firetruck door shut, perturbed that his warm takeout was going to be cold and soggy upon our return.

†

There were four police cars parked every which way outside of the downtown pharmacy. It didn't occur to me until we arrived that there shouldn't have been any customers inside the pharmacy at that hour. That thought caused my heart to drop into my stomach, narrowing the list of possible victims. The chief amongst those being my Sunday School teacher and friend, Joseph Simm. Unconsciously, I ran up to the building and blew right through the outer ring of police officers.

At the epicenter of the scene, I found Jenny again taking photos of a corpse, and Henry standing next to her. I said Henry's name as I approached. He turned to me with a forlorn face. Arriving at his side, I looked down and beheld my Sunday School teacher, pierced through with many elongated holes, eviscerated, and a pair fractured legs caught in some kind of steel mechanism!

CHAPTER 3

Marcus Spasmen's Memoirs of Daring and Disquieting Deeds

– June 24th, 2023 (Referencing back to June 23rd, 2023)

The air was not nearly as dank or as foul as I presupposed. Despite being surrounded by dead bodies, my sense of smell was peculiarly unaffected. The perfectly white floor shone through a thick coat of wax with all the brilliance of the long halogen bulbs that progenerated their illumination across the ceiling. I was certain that there wasn't a single shadow anywhere in that large examination room.

"Number four-thousand one-hundred and six... does that mean Dr. Lisby has examined four-thousand one-hundred and six of Allison's deceased already this year? That seems exceptionally high per capita."

Henry didn't lift his head from the manilla folder in his hand. He scanned the document thoroughly, but after a delay of several seconds, he graced me with a response.

"Dr. Lisby is the coroner for Allison, Hytop, Bass, and at least six other rural communities within twenty miles from here." Henry cut a glance my way, as if to ensure that I hadn't done anything uncouth. His supervision was but for a brief moment before lowering his gaze again to the page. "So, yeah he sees a fair number of dead bodies."

Silently wrapping my fingers around the polished silver handle of one of twelve square doors along an extensive wall, I responded casually to keep Henry's suspicions at rest.

"Well, that makes sense. I was imagining that Allison would be a ghost town if his catalogue of guests was entirely comprised of—"

"SMACK!"

Instantly, the back of my head stung, as if pricked by a piece of metal

and then broadsided by a stack of papers!

"Mark!" Henry barked at the back of my head.

Rubbing my injury, I turned around to see Henry looming over me with the face of a teacher who'd had enough of their most rambunctious youth.

Two sounds clanged simultaneously. One was akin to a locker swinging open. The other more like the release of a push bar on a heavy door.

I looked over Henry's shoulder to see through the narrow window of the exam room door a small round head sprinkled with a few desperate white hairs bobbing in closer. I opened my mouth to speak, but then I saw Henry's eyes widen in a hybrid sort of intermingled anger and dread. It was like when an older sibling realizes that the younger has done something to earn them both a spanking.

"SHUNK!"

Sliding metal came to a heavy stop at the end of its track. I almost jumped out of my skin at the sound. Stepping back to face the noise shoulder to shoulder with Henry, I understood my friend's aghast expression.

A spindly old man whom I didn't recognize was naked and laid out on what appeared to be a long, pullout drawer. A little strip of paper was tied to his left big toe. We stood motionless for a moment, then Henry quickly grabbed the end of the drawer and tried to slide it back into the wall.

The deceased man was about halfway back into his hole when we heard a thin, rattling voice.

"I see you've met the late Dr. Calvin Borginsky. *Ahem* He was a noteworthy astrologist and author. A humble student of science all the days of his life. Pity."

We simultaneously turned to see the speaker retching a wheezing cough into his handkerchief.

Henry stood erect and with as much professionalism as he

could muster, "Dr. Lisby, I apologize for thi—"

"SHUNK!"

I squeezed my eyes shut and held my breath for a few seconds. When I opened my eyes again, Henry's face appeared to be permanently scrunched with an exceptional crimson color. If Henry were a computer, his Control+ALT+Delete bypass had stalled out.

To subdue the tension and give my friend a moment to reboot, I stepped forward with an extended hand.

"Dr. Lisby, it is an honor, sir! My name is Mar—"

"Mark Spasmen... yes, I've heard of you, young man. Quite the student yourself, I gather."

"Well, thank you sir." I gave an appreciative smile and nod, but honestly, I wasn't sure whether to be bothered at his misaddress of "Mark" and not "Marcus" or to be happy that a distinguished doctor and coroner would know who I was and pay heed to my intellectual reputation.

Metal slid over its bearings again and an audible click confirmed the drawer's security at rest.

"CLANK" went the door, and Henry turned to us, wiping his hands to rid himself of embarrassment. It was a fruitless practice, because there was a tense silence for the next few seconds.

Thankfully, Dr. Lisby was ready to move on without a second thought.

"Joseph Zachary Simm; age: forty-seven; height: five feet and nine inches; weight at time of death: one hundred and seventy-four pounds."

Dr. Lisby grabbed a long rolling cart and dragged it behind him as he slowly made his way to the last drawer on the wall of twelve doors.

"No medical history besides hypertension. Joseph's only genetic disposition is a father who had congestive heart failure. Alas, my findings pay little heed to his history."

He clicked open the last shining square door and gently pulled another long drawer out. I vaguely recognized the cadaver upon it, but judging by Henry's pained eyes, he knew better of the corpse.

The doctor added. "I will say that I haven't seen injuries like these for quite some time. Only a brutish beast could assail his fellow man with such cruelty."

Dr. Lisby rolled his cart beside the drawer and used a foot lever to lower the cart beneath the height of the extension.

"When you say 'beast', are you implying that the murderer could be a wild animal that somehow broke into the pharmacy and butchered Mr. Simm?" I asked with broad curiosity, and maybe a touch of playful inquisitiveness.

With a wheezing chuckle, Dr. Lisby responded, "No, young Mark" (my eyes narrowed at the second misaddress), "I don't imagine that any creature beneath the stewardship of mankind could so intentionally, so precisely..." (he paused for a moment to look each of us in the eye) "so malevolently inflict these injuries."

We kept eye-contact for a moment, then he robotically latched the shelf holding Simm to the cart. With the swipe of his hand, another latch gave way and the body was rolling across the room, atop the cart.

"I suppose there are a few animals that could devastate the flesh with similar ferocity. A bear, perhaps?" His voice trailed off.

I didn't acknowledge it till after the fact, but since he had begun to answer my formerly playful question, my skin began to crawl and my heart steadily sank in my chest. However, at the utterance of the word "bear", Henry's eyes and mine flashed at one another, and we experienced a mutual shivering of spines.

I shook my head and returned to the doctor.

"Ah, but I don't think that's the case here." He reassured with a casual motion that clamped the wheels of the cart in place.

"This death was dealt by human hands and that with a rather unnatural utensil."

The top section of the cart married to sliding brackets from the main autopsy table and with all the effort of one feeble hand, Dr. Lisby had shifted the one-hundred-and-seventy-four-pound body into its place for examination.

"Well-trained hands, I'd wager. Come closer, gentlemen."

Henry's face was rather pale, but he looked to me, nodded and we advanced toward the table together.

"Torture was the name of the game for this one. The depraved monster ensnared and then toyed with his victim for quite some time."

I heard a forceful exhale from Henry's nostrils, and subtly noted his watery eyes with my askance look.

"You still have the photos from the scene, Henry?"

"Yes sir." Henry handed him the manilla folder that had just been used to drum me over the head.

"You see, the trap was held under tension here." Dr. Lisby pointed out with a crooked index finger to the first photo.

"The killer concealed the treadplate here," he pointed to a section of the floor mat that was wrinkled up.

"A devastating direct blow across both tibias was sufficient to instantly cripple Mr. Simm." He then pointed to the corpse next to us and the splintered shin bones that protruded through mulched muscle and skin.

At last, I was able to get a close-up view of Simm's injuries. The mangled legs were hard to look at but were honestly the least compelling of his wounds. Simm's abdomen and chest were littered with oblong holes. The perforations were not uniform or monochromatic, but the tissue that bordered the wounds was either black and red, or white, black and red, as if flesh had been pierced then cooked. Three dozen or so of these cauterizing holes littered the poor man's frame. There was also a large slash cut across the side of the deceased's stomach, where his intestines partially protruded. I'm sure that my face displayed disgust for these findings and disbelief at the existence of a monster who could deal them.

Looking at Simm's face, I saw a long, blackened cut from his left ear, crossing down to the right side of his chin. The lips were divided at the razor line of the slash.

I had forgotten to breathe for several seconds while studying this phenomenon, but when I finally did... I realized that I must provide an addendum to my previous claim of the olfactory state of the room.

It was when I took that overdue breath that something tinged along the back of my mind: a faint familiarity. I cocked my head sideways and turned to Henry with one eyebrow raised.

For his part, Henry was as pale as a ghost, trying his utmost to remain standing through the introduction of the autopsy.

This time, I took an intentionally weighty sniff, despite the air's offensive qualities. The picture in the back of my mind began refocusing from its former obscurity.

"You see here, the primary tool in this crime appears to be some type of brand, perhaps with a sharpened edge."

I paid the words little heed, as my investigation took its own direction. I kept sniffing to elucidate my recognition, but with my eyes, I studied one of the deeper perforations. The width of the hole, the size of the narrow, yet distinct insertion jogged my visual memory. Albeit supposedly arbitrary, I realized that the holes in Mr. Simm's torso looked exactly in shape to the deep hole I found in the woods behind Adam's... no Henry's house.

That thought sent my heart into palpitations, not because of any case-related evidence but thinking of the reappearing crater sent me back into my own existential crisis that I had been feverishly trying to avoid.

It was then that another distracting recollection hit me: the scent on Simm's body! It was the same smell from a case that was months prior.
However, those victims were much smaller.

"It does make one wonder why there are no signs of strugg—" "The squirrels!" I said in a tone that was all but shouting.

"I beg your pardon?" Dr. Lisby requested; too confused to be offended at the interruption.

Excitedly, I repeated the exclamation to Henry.

His head was cocked to the side and his mouth hung open in bewilderment, but before he could say a word, his phone started to ring.

"Excuse me, Dr. Lisby. I'm sorry, but I need to take this." Henry stepped away into the antechamber.

"Now what was it you were saying, dear boy?"

Dr. Lisby proceeded to put on heavy rubber gloves.

"I was saying that the smell on his body, of cauterized flesh made me think of anot—"

Henry re-entered the room.

"Mark, we've gotta go. They have the video."

Dr. Lisby turned and asked Henry, "Must you leave so soon? We were about to begin."

Henry looked regretfully at the doctor, then glanced at the gleaming scalpel in his gloved hands. Henry took a deep gulp and responded with hasty respect.

"Typically, I would prefer to stay. I always learn something during your assessments." Henry paused, then looked at the body on the table. He swallowed a boulder-sized lump in his throat and then resumed his regrets, "But I think this situation demands my immediate attention. Thank you, Dr. Lisby."

With that, Henry retreated once more through the double doors without a second's delay.

I hadn't even moved from the spot. The doctor turned to look at me. I smiled back awkwardly, unsure of what to say. He gave a contented grin and moved the knife toward Simm's chest.

"Thank you for your time, doctor." Was my hasty valediction before clearing the same portal and chasing Henry down the hallway.

†

I ducked under the yellow crime scene tape and stayed right on Henry's heels. Two other officers dismissively shook their heads at me from the front door of the pharmacy. Henry and I made our way to the back office, where Simm's work laptop was located. I leaned directly over the computer, claiming first dibs at viewing the murder footage.

"Mark, if you touch ANYTHING you will be back across the tape and out on the street. Got it?" Henry warned.

I submitted with raised hands.

"Hey, you don't have to worry about me, bud. I'll sheathe these lethal weapons." With a wink, I tucked my hands in my pockets.

Henry moved the cursor over the "Play" icon and turned the volume up. I glanced overhead and caught another look of resentment from the curious officers. I gave them a churlish smirk, then returned my eyes to the computer screen.

Oh, how my arrogance was soon to be squashed by an unannounced return to days of inexplicable trepidation.

We both stared at an unmoving screen for several seconds. I was on the verge of mocking Henry for his technological deficiencies, assuming that he hadn't hit "Play" when we finally heard the sound of a deadbolt sliding loose. My attention focused on the glass-paned door at the front of the pharmacy. A dark silhouette passed through the opened portal and promptly turned around to secure the deadbolt.

Once that task was completed, the silhouette advanced into the room. As soon as he had tread two steps into the midst of the floor mat, a flash of metal glinted into view before showing an unnatural bend in the shadow's lower frame, where I would presume was the height of Simm's shins that I knew had been mangled.

The concussive snapping and crunching sound nearly blew out the small laptop speakers. The crunch was so audible and unsettling that one of the two cops who had knelt and was prodding the contraption with his gloved hand, stood upright again with a curse.

"Damn!" He let out while withdrawing the corners of his lips downward. This action revealed his dip-stained bottom teeth.

I spun my head around to see the effect this had on my dearest friend.

Henry's lips were pressed tight together and angled in a small frown. His eyes squinted, but he made no sound.

Come to think of it, neither did the victim. My attention returned to the video.

Simm rocked back and forth on the floor, his legs angled in unnatural fixations. He strained, reaching out to his injuries, but then fell back again, repeating the process compulsively. The man was in shock.

These agonizing motions repeated for a minute or so. After that time, they began to lessen in energy. No sound was heard, apart from his periodic desperate inspiration.

I don't think Henry, himself, had breathed for that entire minute. He watched on, as steady as stone. I couldn't help but blatantly observe my friend's response for several moments.

It was just when I noticed a sharp shift in Henry's eyes to the bottom-right corner of the screen that a faint scuff of rubber against the smooth paint of the concrete floor was audible. We both fixated on that darkest corner of the screen.

Out of the shadows, closest to the security camera, another figure moved forward. The movements were smooth, like a serpent's swift progress. Little effort was behind the disturbing advance. In a moment, the shadow was stooping over Simm. The victim leaned face down on his elbows, but didn't even attempt a retreat. He couldn't. His legs were useless, and his exit was locked at a height that he couldn't reach. The assassin stomped down on the back of Simm's leg with another audible crack. We all winced as we heard the poor man finally uttered a cry.

The shadow tilted its head, as if studying the injured man like a strange insect. Then he wrenched Simm's arm and laid him flat on his back. A small necklace flashed with a glint of silvery light. Simm laid the back of his head on the ground, too weak to prop himself anymore. The silvery light was a small cross necklace that gleamed on his chest.

His predator stood upright, seeming to grow taller with a finalized malevolent purpose. Simm's chest was visibly rising and falling. Henry and I leaned close to not forsake a detail.

Just then, a flash of orange and white soared aloft, as if withdrawn from the waistband of the cruel shadow and then it descended like a missile. The missile sank; every bit of the orange glow concealing within Simm's abdomen. The process repeated with a brief sizzle every time just before the killer would withdraw the knife. Simm wailed aloud from within the darkness. He could no longer suppress the agony.

I was so discomforted at the scene that I found myself leaning away from the screen while I witnessed this man simultaneously get stabbed and burned again and again and again.

The torture seemed to excite the killer, because he then took the knife and slashed Mr. Simm across the face out of shear rapture. The wounds we had just seen at the morgue were now given a source. We just hadn't... identified that source very clearly.

With an ignorant delay, I finally considered how much worse it must be for Henry to have to watch this footage. Glancing inconspicuously, I observed tinges of light trickling down Henry's face, reflecting the hue of the computer screen. While the brutalizing continued, periodic sniffs snuck out from my counterpart.

I lifted my eyes to the two cops across the room. They wore their sorrow plainly as they observed their superior suffering. It bothered me that I didn't feel as sorrowful as they. Shouldn't I be feeling more? It is tragic, but why do I feel so... dispassionate? I mean, a man— no, not just a man. My friend's friend was galvanized before our eyes, and I lack the human decency to regret the loss. Perhaps past traumas have jaded me from feeling remorse. I will need to investigate these emotional incongruencies at a later date.

Looking to the screen, I observed the shade, at last, stand upright. He rolled his shoulders and audibly sighed with relief. It was as if he had just taken the last bite and sat back from a hearty meal. When he stepped aft a pace, we were afforded a view of the now mutilated corpse that we'd met earlier in the morgue.

The murderer steered his right shoulder toward the direction of the office. The rest of his slender form followed. When the lethal weapon came into plain view, Henry sucked in a gasp. I shot a look his direction to see what gave him such anxiety, but he didn't say anything. To my bewilderment, Henry didn't move at all.

"Hey bro?" I asked. "What are you doing?"

I looked to the other officers to see if they understood Henry's game, but they were equally rigid.

Wide-eyed, I repeatedly whipped my head from the two to the one and despite my best efforts, all words failed me. Henry's shocked face kept staring at the screen. Steadily sinking in my dread at the inexplicable, I traced the route of his last concern and looked to the computer.

The murderer stood, facing the rear of the building, somewhere beneath the camera's perspective. As I continued to view the recording, my mind stung with the flash of some image that seared to recall.

In his hand, the damning weapon that he used to kill Simm proved to be a dagger, pulsating orange, black, and white, like currents of magma churning within a volcano. Somehow, I knew that I had seen this before, but I couldn't quite place where. This should have seemed like an inconsequential detail in the midst of reality being immobilized before me. The only thing that still moved besides myself was the recorded fall of small magmatic drips upon the ground beside where the murderer stood. My gaze again fixated on the death-dealing tool.

"It was a gift, you know?"

I leaned in close and maxed out the volume on the computer speaker.

"I thought it befit him for all those years of loyal service."

The growling voice got slightly louder, as if the murderer's audience was somewhere in the back office.

"He showed such potential."

This time, the voice was unfathomably deep, like the resounding rumble of a bull alligator. I even reached to turn the volume back down. In doing so, I noticed the figure steadily approaching the back of the pharmacy, blade dripping in sizzling flashes with each step. The sound of the sizzles seemed to be blaring from the computer speaker.

"He just... lacked patience."

My hair began to stand on end after the speaker finished these words. It was then that I realized something smelled like it was burning!

"I see now what he tried to hoard for himself. How foolish of him to think he could hide it from us..."

This time I felt his words reverberate in my chest. That sonorous resonance was somewhere in the room with me!

I lifted my eyes above the computer desk and saw pops of flame jump from the ground, in constantly decreasing proximity. Little fires were igniting across the floor and headed my direction! I knew that I needed to do something. The others were all paralyzed, and those incipient flames would soon overtake them.

I happened to look down again and suddenly made a mortifying connection. Every time that a splash of lava dropped from his knife in the video, a spot of the floor in the present room would ignite! I kept watching in horror and confusion. My brain could not adapt to this nightmarish phenomenon. It all reached a climax when the lengthening trail extended to just in front of the computer desk. I looked at the screen again and could see that the shadow was gone!

"Or hide you from me, Marcus."

If words could consume, those would have!

I felt his breath chill my neck into a flurry of goosebumps and every instinct in my body told me to run. I, however, unknowingly joined the ranks of the immobile. I was doomed to simply stand still and be consumed!

"I would commend him for his choice in vessel." The voice rumbled behind my ear.

"You reek of torment."

That remark concluded with a heavy sniffing sound, like that of a dog.

"Your face seeps with doubt."

A frigid chill was emanating around the side of my head, but I couldn't turn to look. My petrified eyes widened to see whatever I could steal a glimpse of. Nothing but a human shape, cloaked in blackness leaned uncomfortably close to my face in sadistic intimacy.

After an unbearable duration, the cold receded.

"I won't deceive you, Marcus. You aren't special. There's a world full of resentful skeptics. You're just the closest tool for the task. You're like a nail within reach: convenient and disposable.

"It benefits you that the task is so near at hand. If we were elsewhere, I'd slit your throat and drink all of your blood while warming my mortal frame by the fire of your burning corpse. You mean nothing to me, Marcus. You and your supremely meddlesome friend here would be dead right now, if it weren't more convenient to employ your existence otherwise."

He raised the glowing dagger.

"Then again, you humans are so expendable. I could just kill all four of you and burn this place to the ground. Maybe... start fresh tomorrow with some other oblivious skeptic."

He pressed the knife against my neck! Blood began to pound in my head, and my breathing heaved, but I still could not move! A faint searing sound rose, like a steak on the griddle. My chest also began to burn, like a brand pressed upon it. The scar that Lionel gave me ached, as if it was being carved anew!

"Indeed, the longer we speak, the more your skepticism wanes."

I couldn't catch my breath as all my attention was fixed on saving myself from this torture! I could feel the tightness of my skin give way to a razor's edge and the pulse of blood to a wetting wound. The burning continued to intensify. The stench of burnt iron rose in the air. The whole right side of my neck began to quiver under the heat. Everywhere throbbed, except the spot where the knife had directly touched. All those nerves were dead.

"But why waste an unbent nail?"

He lowered the dagger from my neck, then I saw in my

periphery that he casually aimed it at Henry, flicking drops of ember onto his jacket.

"Even this faithful wretch will serve our purpose."

The flames crept to life, slowly expanding on Henry's jacket.

"No Marcus, my convenient little nail. You will live today, but don't forget that I hold you in my hand, and in the proper time, you will be buried deep; sealing the purpose that is even greater than I. In the end, you will see."

I heard the sound of metal sliding into its rest and the fading tap of receding steps.

"I'll see you very soon, my little nail."

Suddenly, I felt free to move. I spun around to see if the killer was behind me. The empty wall confirmed that he was gone. Then my thoughts returned to the others.

I could hear Henry say, "What the? Augh!" As he patted out the growing flames on his jacket!

Curses flew out from across the room, as the two other officers found themselves surrounded by a heightening blaze!

"Mark, we've got to get out of here!" Henry cried.

"Tommy! Carlyle! Let's move!"

Henry yanked me by the sleeve of my shirt and we sprinted around the office desk and across the pharmacy floor. Tommy and Carlyle had managed to retreat from the flames. All of us instinctively crouched as we made the way for the door. Smoke had filled the store so we blindly felt for the push bar.

"Here!" Henry yelled, and with a group effort, we all crashed forward out the door. By the time we had hit the sidewalk, the interior of the store blazed in a rolling wall of orange. The windows began to blacken. Henry yanked my shoulder again, and we sprinted across the street.

Henry keyed up his radio: "Dispatch Fire to Simm's Drugs."

Henry stood with a heaving chest, his eyes transfixed on the burning building. We were all stunned for several seconds. I studied those flames for several moments, unable to look away. Unthinking, I reached for my neck.

A new pain tore at my throat when I withdrew my hand.

A clump of ashen skin stuck to my fingers as blood oozed down my arm. I began to feel weak.

"Mark? What is that?" Henry asked, with palpable dread in his voice.

I fell backward and my vision began to fade as Henry cried out my name once again. His voice echoing somewhere from the other end of a long black tunnel.

Henry Loadwain's Letter to Misty Loadwain – 24 June 2023

Well, as you heard on the phone call this morning, Mark is doing much better. I haven't left his side, despite answering a dozen calls from everyone trying to understand what happened last night.

The truth is, I really can't explain anything. I sort of... lost control. Well, not really lost control, but it was almost like I was asleep or absent in some strange way. A kind of black out. I've never blacked out, because I think that usually looks more like a fainting spell. This was so weird because one moment, I'm looking at the recording of the crime and the next, I'm trying to pat out a fire that's burning holes in my jacket. Meanwhile, the room in front of me is going up in flames. Thank God we all made it, but Mark somehow got burned... or cut... or... both. I guess a jagged piece of heated metal caught him on the way out. He's been sedated while they treated his wound, but when he wakes up, I'm gonna have a pile of questions for him.

The last thing I remember is watching that... that monster turn away from Joseph's gnarled body, then—

Misty, I now remember what I saw!

But how? That knife should be gone. All of Id's weapons were destroyed. How? There's no way Id is still alive! I watched him die.

So, who could have found that knife, if it wasn't consumed in the beam? I'm sitting here, looking at Mark recover from his wounds, thinking that his neck might not have been snagged by rubble, after all.

Neither Tommy nor Carlyle have any memory either. Their first thoughts after blacking out are similar to mine. That just leaves Mark as the only witness to what really happened before Simm's store burned to the ground.

I'll be posted right here until he is strong enough to share his side of the story.

In other news, I called Bryce and Cynthia Spasmen as soon as we got to the hospital. I made them aware of Mark's condition. I'm very prompt nowadays, to notify his parents whenever Mark takes one of these trips to near-death experience, given that Mrs. Cynthia tore me a new one for not notifying her of Mark's involvement in the Id affair.

I don't think Mark has even dared show them the scar on his chest. I'd wager that he'll try to keep that concealed from them for the rest of his life.

✝

I've sat for a while writing this letter while biding my time. The doctor said that Mark's anesthesia should wear off soon. So, before any other bizarre things happen, I want to make sure that I've slowed down enough to tell you what I need to say.

I'm sorry, Misty. I'm sorry for how cold I've been. It's just... so much has happened. I've lost so much in the last eight months. I know... we've both lost so much.

I'm sorry that I haven't been a better comforter to you. It is to my fault that when I'm hurting, I pull away. When we are both hurting, I try to deal with it myself and I lose sight of your pain. I'm so selfish. I've pushed my feelings down; again, and again. In doing so, I've pushed your feelings down, too. Apparently, I'm too afraid to face your pain, because I'd then have to acknowledge my own.

Misty, you're the most important person in the world to me, and I'm failing miserably at showing it. Please forgive me. I want to do better. I want to love you better. Please be patient with me.

I don't wanna ramble on talking about myself, but I need to trust you with my feelings. So here goes an attempt at being vulnerable!

One thing that I've struggled with is that I've had to step into Isaac's role, and I'm nowhere near the man he was. I don't know how to run a department. I'm too young, but everyone looks to me now. What am I supposed to do? What if I fail? What if they see my weaknesses, my inability to perform the way Isaac did? What if my error costs someone else their life? I've already seen too many friends die. I don't know if I could live with that.

Speaking of Joseph, at first, I wasn't too disturbed. I kept my stern game-face when we went to the coroner. It was surreal to see my brother-in-Christ, pale and lifeless, laying on the same table that I've seen many strangers examined on. My mind couldn't really register that it was him. It looked like him, but he wasn't there. I mean, I know he wasn't spiritually there, but it even felt like the body didn't belong to him.

I don't know... I know that sounds crazy.

But later, when we were watching the recording (which is no longer viable evidence), I heard his dying voice. I watched him suffer. It all hit me then, and I was filled with hatred for his killer. I don't know who this filth is, but I pray that somebody else arrests him before I find him. I'm not quite sure what I'd do if we met alone in a dark alley. I know I shouldn't even think like that, but it's hard not to want to kill the guy who butchered your friend.

"Vengeance is mine, I will repay,' says the Lord." God will have His vengeance. Help me, Lord, to believe that.

Mark is finally waking up. Time for some answers! Misty, I love you more than life itself! I hope this letter is clearer than my mind trying to write it!

-    Love, Henry

Private Journal of Grigory Yakor (25 June '23)

Well, yesterday was just about the polar opposite of last shift. We had no calls during the day and only one at night (слава Богу), and that call was just a medical call, so it didn't demand too much of my precious sleep. However, it sounds like A-Shift had an eventful night. Willard told me, at length, about the fire they had at *Simm's Drugs*. Mark was there with Henry when it happened. Apparently, they were reviewing the footage of the murder when a second trap was set off and an electrical fire started. At least, that's Mark's side of the story. He's the only one of the witnesses who had a coherent story.

If they had all blacked out, I would think that some kind of chemical exposure took place, but Mark never reported blacking out. He just described flames springing up from behind the computer. It could have just been faulty wiring, but this is Allison... so it was probably a trap.

Last night's run on the firetruck was a domestic call. Some loser reportedly punched his girlfriend, then fled the scene. Coward. Sadly, I've been to too many calls like that. Spineless worms think that they are strong because they can boss a woman around, beating her if she doesn't listen. I'd like to "assist" such scum-bags right down a flight of stairs. Anyway, we had to wait for PD to secure the scene... of course. (That protocol alone is Henry's favorite topic to prod me with, as he calls us firefighters the "Second Responders.") I'm digressing...

So, we get on scene and Gamble is already there, shining his flashlight on the offended woman's wounds. She had a busted lip and her left eye was swollen shut. The bleeding from her lip had all but stopped by now. We began to ask her what happened when APD's CSI car pulled up and Jenny O'Donnel stepped out.

"What the Hell is she doing here?" Gamble exhaled in complaint.

She walked up, eyeing Gamble closely before moving right on past him and approaching the patient. She didn't say a word, but stood still, watching the bruised woman, then glancing back to Gamble.

I ignored the tension between the officers and resumed my patient history gathering.

"Are you taking any medications for hypertension?"

"Hyper-what?"

"Sorry, I mean, high blood pressure."

"Oh, naw. No, nothin' like that."

"Did you ever lose consciousness during—"

I didn't even hear myself finish the question. I was too distracted by the altercation brewing behind me.

"This is open and shut. I don't even see why you need to be here, right now." Gamble growled.

"Because... we are trying to tie together any other possible leads to the Simm Investigation."

"Oh, right like this dumb hussy has any connection to your mysterious 'Trapper', or whatever you are calling him."

The patient gasped and my eyes widened in disbelief at Gamble's lack of couth.

"If y'all don't mind taking your lovers' spat elsewhere." I suggested through clenched teeth.

"Ugh, what is with you?" Jenny asked in disgust.

"You know what? Go to Hell. Y'all have fun playing 'CSI: Allison,'" he indicated with quotation fingers before retreating to his patrol car and slamming the door.

Jenny continued to look around the property, taking photos of spots where the patient's boyfriend threw her down, or where he punched her, etc. In no time, Jenny had photographed almost every facet of the double-wide trailer and the surrounding property.

My patient chose to be transported by ambulance and treated at the hospital. We returned to service and to bed.

†

I'm at JMS today, and the day on the ambulance has been equally uneventful. It's great to have some downtime to relax and clear my mind, but the superstitious firefighter in me is setting off warning signals that peace will soon come to an abrupt end.

I've been doing a lot of research the past two days. Not EMS research, or Russian news, or weightlifting, but rings. Yes, my children, engagement rings! Lia is surely the one I intend to spend the rest of my life with. I've never been more challenged, strengthened, and supported by any other human.

Lia is wise and filled with faith beyond her years. She's beautiful. She's constantly intentional and patient. She may be a little hesitant and anxious at times, but perhaps it's good for me to be with somebody who thinks things through a little more. Despite her tendencies to be apprehensive, she has been forward in implying that she wants us to be more than girlfriend and boyfriend.

I know it sounds cliché, but I have never felt this way about any other person before. When I was young and had just moved to the United States, I thought that I would be alone forever. No one would want to marry a pale, gangly, boy from Russia with a thick accent. That concern only heightened in the wake of recent world events that would cause Russian-Americans to be deemed unwelcomed intruders. Lia didn't care about any of that. She was looking for things that permanently defined my character. She was studying my soul, to see if she could trust it.

Praise God, she has! And I… I think I'm ready to trust hers as well.

The greatest irony is that when I finally stopped worrying about finding a mate, God provided who I believe to be the perfect one. I can only daydream what marriage would be like, but whether it's like walking on clouds or drudging through bogs, there is no one I'd rather be with than Lia.

All that lovey-dovey, metaphysical musing aside, I've still got to find the perfect ring. She's just happened to show me a few unique styles out of "idle" appreciation when one pops up on her phone. Of course, the targeting advertisements on her social media wouldn't be showing them if that wasn't a topic of interest to her.

She says that she'd just be happy to be married to me, regardless of the way the ring looks. Well, I won't let that be the reason to settle for a half-hearted effort of an engagement ring. It may be undue pressure that I'm putting on myself, but Lia is worthy of—

— Got to go, the tones just went off and there's been a possible murder at the police department!

The Third Hunt

I've always taken a particular fancy to assailing the avian amidst flight. A beautiful bird flaps and glides with such surety. Its wings have always upheld it. The creature has no need to fear the harsher effects of gravity. Why should it dread the hard earth far below if the lift beneath its feathered limbs has always carried it safely to desired rest?

Perhaps the concussive humbling of my weapon savagely... instantaneously tearing away all that confidence elicits a rare dosage of ecstasy. Oh, how I love to see the proud creatures at last understand how frail they truly are.

This proud little thing saw me coming from a long way off. To her grave regret, she didn't consider me enough of a threat. Tsk tsk... 'tis often simply best to hide in plain sight.

'Tis true, this little dove's death was nonessential, for I harbored no designs to eat my quarry... for the time being, at least. But I could have let the preening creature live, especially since time is fast approaching and my attention is due elsewhere.

Just a few more kills, and then... transcendence!

Oh, I can almost feel the cold grasp of his appreciation on my scalp. Like the affection of a proud father, grasping his son's head. My Lord, I will make you proud.

In truth, it is for the best that I killed this dove. Her awareness and her curiosity were liabilities that I would rather not afford. I have an unblemished record before my Lord. I dare not mar it now.

†

She flitted her wings at my approach and ruffled her feathers, but she did not fly. Her head spun about to see who else was nearby. She was the only bird in the tree. There was no more of her mistaking me for one of her kind. The fear began to grow in her eyes. The urge was rising in her frame to take flight, but she hesitated. Something held her in place; nothing of my doing, but I did take full advantage of it.

In disbelief, she gave a mourning coo and sat in her perch

until I had already encroached well within range to strike. The coos fell silent as the avian prey realized my intent. Horror-stricken silence ensued for some time. The creature didn't see me ready my shotgun, but all too late the dove knew escape was a diminishing hope.

My finger floated motionlessly over the trigger, just begging for the bird to take off and allow it the opportunity to squeeze down on the gavel of her condemnation.

My temporal pulse thumped, not in fear, but in exhilaration. I couldn't suppress the smile any longer. The thought of her life draining was... elating. I longed to hear this one's death cry. I needed it. I needed her blood. The fever came over me.

An abrupt whistle signaled her retreat! She took off to her right, fleeing across the far side of the tree, wings flapping frantically, and whistling in hopes of alarming any other birds that may be nearby. As I said, this was a lonely dove.

I giggled with delight while raising the shotgun to my shoulder and lining up my sights.

One more pronounced whistle was let out. This tune seemed a bit higher pitch, indicating desperation to escape what she already knew to be imminent.

The world shook around us as the gavel of fate fell. A cloud of feathers and bloody mist painted this glorious scene, with a backdrop of a sinking sunset.

I walked up to my prey. The bird's mouth gasped open and closed, but no air passed through. Eyes were fixed forward in a gaze of astonishment. The mouth soon stopped moving. Standing over that disheveled dove, I looked down and drank deep of the hatred that had been pooling in my thoughts of her.

Kneeling beside the lifeless game, I dipped my fingers in her growing pool of blood. The warm fluid seemed to pull up and cling to my skin. I brought my fingers close and sniffed slowly, eyes rolling back in my head. Without a second thought, I put my fingers in my mouth and cleaned them thoroughly. I stayed about this task till I heard the caw and squawk of other birds beginning to encircle, seeking what fate befell this lone dove, perched upon that tree.

Marcus Spasmen's Personal Memoirs - June 26th, 2023

I pushed aside the low-hanging branches that flexed without tension, then ducked beneath other broad, unrelenting ones to work my way to the enigmatic meeting place.

Just before entering the clearing, I stopped short of a waist-high branch, laden with rigid dark green leaves. Looking ahead, I could see Gamble transfixed on some point of the canopy above him.

Socially, I felt inclined to advance and make him aware of my arrival, but something held me back. Some curiosity, perhaps. What sort of thing enraptures the mind of a police officer steeped in solitude? At least, an officer who isn't Henry Loadwain.

But Gamble simply stood there, as if watching for birds, or waiting for fruit to fall from the tree so that he could catch it just in time. Some reflex exercise, perhaps? Young cops are always thinking up ways to enhance their combative edge. He didn't move, however. Nor was there any type of fruit in the tree. He just remained there, hands in his pockets, standing motionless for some time.

Then it hit me. I had seen Henry do the same thing on several occasions.

Disassociation from the environment occurs when someone pays no heed to their surroundings and reflects on past experiences, usually uncomfortable (sometimes even traumatic) ones. It even has the tendency to absorb one's mind in fearful daydreams about possible dangers, regardless of whether that particular threat has been experienced before. It is a fascinating defense mechanism that the mind uses to keep vigilance.

While I was staring and dwelling on these things, I almost missed the fact that Gamble had begun to move from the base of the tree to the center of the clearing.

His hands never left his pockets as he walked. His head full of thick auburn hair was tilted forward, monitoring the steps he took. Beard-shrouded lips were pursed in contemplation as he arrived at the crater that we both had previously marveled over. He continued in this descending posture whilst absently staring, just like he had at the tree moments before.

I began to shift my leg, feeling that it was high time our conversation started, but before my foot lifted from the pine straw, an awful wrenching sound scared the birds nesting in the trees above me.

Startled, I looked ahead to see Gamble leaning forward, hands on his knees and emesis flowing from his mouth. I paused, head cocked to the side, suddenly debating whether I really wanted to approach him now.

"Are you planning on hiding all day? You're stalkin' me like a deer, Marcus." Gamble chuckled, while wiping his lips on his sleeve.

Too late.

"Damnit man, what's come over you? Did you eat some bad oysters?" I asked jokingly, as if it was somehow his fault that he was vomiting.

"No," he forced a laugh with hands on his knees. "I think I'm just fighting off a stomach bug."

"Oh, well in that case. I'll just keep my distance... approximately fifty feet." I too forced a laugh, suppressing my genuine discomfort at meeting in light of his present condition.

Gamble stood upright, acting as if he hadn't just puked his guts out. Standing just close enough to be able to speak without shouting, I gave him a nod, wordlessly asking to ensure that he was going to be alright.

He nodded in return and asked, "So... what did you want to meet about? Would a phone call not have sufficed?"

"Although, I see now that calling you might have been for the best, I felt it imperative that we pick up where we last left off. I mean, we were exploring some pretty substantial findings, and I just don't know how to make sense of it."

Gamble nodded in silence as I continued.

"I know that a lot has gone on since we last met. You all have been incredibly busy, but I've got this existential crater (emphatically straightening my open palms in the direction of the hole) that we discovered, and I don't see how it makes any sense."

Clearing his throat, Gamble lightly coughed then said, "Well, honestly. I hadn't been able to make sense of it either. I guess I've been kind of glad to be busy, in a morbid sort of way. I haven't had to think about what this discovery might mean. In no way, am I accepting Henry's religious excuses about what happened here."

"Oh, well of course not!" I agreed energetically. "Such notions are ludicrous, but this scene does present some very supernatural implications, although it pains me to say it."

Gamble drew in a long breath. "Marcus, I think it's best that we cling tightly to the world around us. We can count on what we experience with our five senses and disregard any faith-based jargon that others might tell us. What do we know for sure about this spot here?"

I looked up at the unchanging hole in the canopy, cut in a perfect circle. I looked down at the morning glories visibly growing and winding about, like gentle tendrils of an anemone. I looked at the leveled woods around us, where no other new plants had grown. My eyes returned to Gamble.

With a resigned scoff, I imploringly looked at him. "Nothing."

"Don't rush to interpret, Marcus. Don't read between the lines."

"That's like telling concrete not to be so stiff."

"Okay. Let me show you."

Gamble took a step closer to me. I was unsettled at the idea of rogue viral molecules vaporizing and floating their way toward me, but he stopped short before getting unacceptably close. He turned about so that we could face the same direction.

"So, we KNOW that something cut a hole in the treetops, and that evidently nothing can grow back. We KNOW that there is a crater, but we DON'T KNOW how those two things were made. We KNOW that something toppled all these trees at the same time. We DON'T KNOW what toppled them. We KNOW that this spot is behind Henry's property, even though we once believed it to be elsewhere. Let's just stay with the tangible. Seek the answers from something tangible. Right?"

"But you make it sound so simple. As if, we shouldn't be surprised by these things at all."

"Well, I'm not sayin' you can't be surprised. I'm just sayin' don't jump to conclusions. You see a couple weird things and retreat back to the idea of a sky-daddy? That tells me that you haven't totally freed yourself from religion."

I chewed on that for several moments.

"How did you do it? Aren't like ninety percent of your coworkers Bible thumpers?"

"Ha-ha. Yeah, which is unusual for cops."

"It fits the bill for Allison, doesn't it?"

Gamble chuckled, "Yeah. We are finding that Allison is…" (he gestured with his hand to the scene around us) "an atypical place."

I thought it encouraging that he said, "We." It gave me a sense of solidarity. Knowing that I wasn't alone in this ethereal quagmire was no small degree of comfort to me.

Gamble continued, "Although, it might benefit us to keep an open mind. I don't want you to think that I'm saying nothing supernatural can happen, just stick to the evidence."

When he finished his statement, my mind flashed to the other night, when I met with that dark figure whose knife dripped like it had just been drawn from a pool of lava. How was I going to explain that one to my pragmatic friend here? I thought it best to try.

"Hey Gamble, there's something else."

He turned toward me, curious eyebrows angulating. "Really?

What else?"

"The other night, I was with Henry at Simm's—"

Gamble's phone interrupted my confession. He put up a finger, indicating that he wanted me to hold the thought.

"Hellooo?" Sustaining the "ooo" sound for relaxed cordiality.

A long pause accompanied with an unnatural stillness gave way to a sharp inhale and an "Oh no," and then "damn." And concluded with a "I'm on my way."

He lowered the phone, looked at me in disbelief and said in a flat tone, "Jenny is dead." He closed his eyes and shook his head.

"Damn." He said again.

"Oh God." I said.

Gamble winced, "See?" He smirked at me and gave a morbid chuckle. Then, without a word, he stormed off through the opening we had begun to carve with our repeated visits.

"Oh no!" I said aloud to the crater and the hole-punched canopy. "Poor Henry."

Adam Clemmens' Prayer Journal – June 27th, 2023

I've just found out that two more people have died here in town. Both were victims to this twisted "Hunter". Personally, I'm convinced that all three recent deaths were in fact murders, even though nothing has been publicly stated about Isaac's death being anything but natural causes. I bet Henry knows. I could ask him. He probably wouldn't tell me, though.

Trust —with Henry— is always one-sided. He expects me to trust him, but he never confides in me... what a hypocrite!

God, did I really just say that?

I hear Your whispers. What would you have me do, Lord?

"Stay away."

Stay away from what? From Henry? But he's like a brother

to me, and he's always striven to be Your faithful servant. Why would I stay away from him?

"Stay away from them."

"Them"? From Henry's friends? But I owe them so much. They saved my life, and they fought to save Merrin's... even though they failed. You had to come in and save us all.

But even You delayed in Your saving of us! Why? Why let us suffer first? Is that kindness? Is that the affection of a "loving God"?

I'm... I'm not sure why I wrote that. Perhaps I should scratch out such blasphemous things. I hope nobody thinks that I'm a faithless coward as they read this.

†

I had to reprimand Merrin again. She went beyond the porch to go and check the mail! How many times do I have to tell her not to leave the porch?

It's... it's not safe for her out there! The Hunter could be anywhere.

"He could have snatched you in an instant. We can't go outside, honey."

She, of course, cried at my reprimand, but safety is more important than comfort, so I chose to ignore her tears. Perhaps it's best to break her heart now but keep her alive forever. Well, not forever...

No, don't let me think about it, Lord. I lost her once! I can't do it again! I can't...

You wouldn't let her die, would you? We've already endured our trial.

"Never."

No, of course You wouldn't. I know You wouldn't. I just needed to hear You say it. This new communion... it's so direct, so clear. And to think that it took separating myself from the "church" community. Are they really Your church if so much has happened to them? Or are they just a convocation of heretics?

"They're all deceivers."

I thought so! Then there really is no grace reserved for them?

Ah! *"Them"*. You said, "Stay away from _them_."

This is what You meant. They are not Your church at all. You want me to stay away from this false congregation then. Very well.

Even Henry, though? That will be difficult, but yes, Lord. It will be done.

†

Owen, too, needed a beating today. He tried to speak to the neighbor's boy, who for only seven years old has fed richly on the lies that the defiled David Kent teaches.

Wait, what lies? What has come over me? I faithfully adhered to the teachings for years. But if You tell me that these things are false, I will make them untrue in my heart, and work to deconstruct these presuppositions.

"It's all lies."

My mind... it still feels in torment. I hear Your whispers and I want to believe, but surely all of the things taught in Scripture can't be false can they?

"They're compromised words."

So, what do I trust, if I don't have Scripture?

"I'm here. Trust in me."

Very well, I will trust in Your whispers. You made Yourself plain to me in that twilight glen, and You are doing so here.

Help me to protect these children from themselves and their insolent disregard for my rules. I can't face the darkness of the night again. I mean... we can't face it.

CHAPTER 4

<u>Marcus Spasmen's Memoirs: Pertaining to the Findings</u>

<u>of Miss O'Donnel's Autopsy – June 27th, 2023</u>

I half expected Henry to move about the room, with his left hand viced down onto my shoulder to prevent me from opening any more corpse cabinets. To my surprise, however, he was not nearly as anxious about my behavior as anticipated. He seemed focused. Solemn, but focused.

Somehow, he seemed more put together today, than he had at the death of Joseph Simm. I thought that strange because he worked with Jenny for years. I imagined that following Simm's death, Henry would crumble at the loss of yet another friend. Today, I was not bashful about eyeing him skeptically.

I grabbed the door handle and pulled, allowing us entry into the examination room, holding it for Henry. I stared with no small measure of inquisitiveness as he passed by, but he walked through without turning.

"Thanks, Mark." He said, in a lighter tone than his face displayed. I just could not get a read on him.

"Ah, hello Henry, and hello young Mark." An already gloved hand waved to us from the far side of the exam table. Dr. Lisby gave us a smile and nod, which was followed by subtle, bobbing continuations that I'm sure he didn't even realize he was doing.

What was the point of changing my name, if nobody was going to use my new nomenclature? I'm afraid I have to admit that I gave a frown upon hearing the third of these consecutive abuses of my moniker. Not only that, he called me "young," but what about Henry? We're practically the same age!

"Henry, I am so sorry to meet under these circumstances.

Jenny was a marvelous young lady, with a heart of gold," consoled the good coroner.

Again, I stared Henry down to study his physiognomy.

Henry pressed his lower lip tight to its proximal twin and gave a few shallow nods as he motioned acceptance of the tragic state of things.

"Thank you. Yes sir, these are hard days, for sure. Jenny was a wonderful person. I will miss her."

Something wasn't quite right. How was he so... resolved?

"Well, if you're ready, gentlemen, we can begin." Dr. Lisby invited with a scalpel in one hand and the free hand reaching toward an old tape recorder resting on a narrow rolling table. He paused with his finger over the most worn button with a half-faded red circle on it, his head turned to Henry. I was motionless, transfixed on the faintest features of my friend's face. I would not miss a single, microscopic expression.

Henry's eyes glistened as he put on gloves and reached out to the cadaver of Jenny O'Donnel. He put his hand on her motionless, pale right shoulder. Neither the doctor nor I made a sound.

Henry kept his arm there and hung his head. The silence ensued and we were all as statues. I allowed myself a moment to glance from Henry, and I briefly observed the coroner, so I might understand what is the appropriate decorum for such moments. His gloved hands were held together, and hanging low, but ensuring not to touch anything. Dr. Lisby just looked on peacefully, unashamed to stare at Henry's grieving. It was a powerful scene that he must have been a part of thousands of times.

How strange for this man to know the intimate connections of countless lives, to see the weight of tragedy repeatedly, and yet be unfazed. This man has spent more time with death, than anyone in any other profession. I imagine that it would be easier for him to just look at Jenny as a sack of bone and sinew, but instead he finds peace in acknowledging the pain that others feel, and remains tranquil with the irrevocable demands of mortality.

Even though I've seen more gruesome things than most, I simply have to look at a dead body and chills will run up my spine.

Where did Dr. Lisby's tranquility come from? Speaking of tranquility, Henry at last raised his head, and simply said, "Ok." With that, Dr. Lisby pressed his finger down on the "record" button and proceeded with his autopsy. We remained silent and listened attentively throughout the entire process.

Periodically, I checked on Henry. He studied the cadaver with hawk-like observation. He furiously scribbled onto his legal pad when Dr. Lisby mentioned that the ammunition retrieved from her shoulder and face was birdshot, not buckshot or slugs. He also noted the doctor's description of vital organs struck by the pellets, including her carotid artery, which could very well have been the damning strike.

Despite nearly gagging when I saw the subject's stomach placed on a metal dish, I held my ground through it all. After removing the liver and placing it in its own tray, the doctor lifted his eyes in my direction and asked if I was "quite alright?" I nodded enthusiastically, despite the urge to succumb to my nausea.

Henry's notetaking was interspersed through the rest of the examination. By the time that Dr. Lisby removed his gloves and pressed the "stop" button Henry flipped his notepad closed with a definitive snap. In a strong voice, like that of a ready warrior, Henry said, "Thank you for all you do, Dr. Lisby."

At that, he began to walk out the door. I was unable to move just yet. Something glued me to the spot. Despite the grotesque scene of disembowelment, I couldn't take my eyes from the examination table.

"Ah, Henry!" Dr. Lisby called, just before Henry reached the push bar of the door. "These are the results of the autopsy of Chief Knox." He said, extending a rather thick manilla folder. "I imagine you'll have some questions. My cell phone number is on a note card tucked inside."

My friend's face betrayed confusion.

"Autopsy?"

"It seems Miss O'Donnel felt something irregular about the circumstances regarding his death. She submitted the order the following day, but kept the request exclusive between the two of us."

Henry continued listening while gripping the documents.

"Given her sorrowful and untimely demise, I deem it best to entrust this information to you."

Dr. Lisby cast a wary glance in my direction, but it passed in a blink.

Henry seemed stunned. He opened his mouth to speak, then closed it again silently. After a lengthy pause, Henry finally spoke, "Thank you, sir." He made an immediate about-face and resumed his departure.

I had yet to move. After a few seconds of silence, I heard the old man's voice directed at me.

"Such is our own path soon enough. Best make peace with that, young man."

I looked past the exposed contents of the chest cavity, to observe the ashen face of Jenny one more time, with its hemispheric division of one side unblemished and the other peppered with holes. Then, my eyes were drawn again to the raw flesh.

"How can I?"

Dr. Lisby approached with a paper towel, drying his freshly cleaned hands. He squeezed my shoulder and answered in his rattly voice.

"Oh, I think you already know the answer. Don't you... Mark?" At that, he winked and turned away. "Have a blessed day, young man." He said aloud to the rest of the empty room.

I turned and followed Henry's retreat without a parting word.

†

I stepped out onto the entrance steps of the morgue. Henry was already in his Crown Vic and reviewing the file that Dr. Lisby had given him. I thought to go to the window but considered that he might need some time alone to recover from the gruesome examination.

I made my way toward the car when I heard the faint sound of a window sliding open.

I turned to see Henry beckon with a nod to the window. He was smiling. How was he smiling?

"Are you ok, Henry?"

"Yeah bud, thank you." He nodded with another sober smile.

His face was showing a stillness that didn't fit the emotional barrage he'd withstood thus far. I was convinced that he was lying to himself.

I knew that if I dug deep enough, I would be able to get my fingernails underneath and peel off this façade. As long as he avoided the pain, he would never properly heal. What kind of friend would I be if I just stood by and let Henry spiral downward into a pit of self-destructive repression.

"But are you really, my friend? It would be a perfectly tenable notion if you were not 'OK.'"

"Well, I'm not saying that I'm not having a tough time, or that I'm not grieving. I'm just... anchored."

"Anchored?"

"Yeah, I'm definitely hurting. I've lost so many friends, but I'm at peace. I trust in God's plan."

My skepticism began to flare up within me, like a match that had been struck amidst a pitch-black room. I almost pursed my lips and raised my eyebrow to signify marked incredulity, but I caught myself. This was not the time to mock Henry's sanctimonious platitudes. If his delusion was helping him handle his emotions, I wasn't going to abash him for it. As long as his religion allowed him to face his feelings; that wasn't my immediate concern. However, I felt it my duty to inquire a little more about his anchoring.

"I'm glad you are calm and 'anchored' as you say, but I want to make sure that you are allowing yourself a chance... well, more likely *chances* to feel all the emotions that you need to feel.

"I mean, I'm just a little concerned, because you were

obviously hurting when your chief passed away. Then, I know it hurt to see you lose Mr. Simm. It was worse, having to watch him be killed."

Henry's face grew forlorn, and he nodded sorrowfully.

"Then Miss O'Donnel gets tragically murdered, and now... something has changed. I mean, you cared about her too, right? You're sad to see her gone, too, right?"

"If you'd believe it, Mark, her death is even harder to deal with than the others'."

"Really? But you're much more composed now than you were at first. What's changed?"

"I've talked to Him about it."

"Who? Dr. Lisby?"

"No", Henry answered with a soft smile.

"Well... Grigory, Gamble, Adam, the Hunter, for crying out loud? Who?"

Pain and anger flashed through Henry's face at the mention of the murderer's title. Then he lowered his head and took a deep breath.

"No, Mark. I've finally paused and talked to *Him* about it."

Annoyed at the return to the topic of God, I responded with pointed sarcasm.

"Really? What did He say?" I asked rhetorically, anticipating that Henry would then have to admit that God didn't actually commune back with him.

"He reminded me to be still; to trust in His timing. He told me that vengeance was His, and that He would repay. He told me to cast my cares upon Him, because He cares about me."

I recognized these scriptural snippets, which then only fueled my vexation. He was using Bible references in lieu of actually hearing anything from God.

"Henry... these are just passages from the Bible. I thought you said that God spoke to you."

I knew that this was not the time to be hostile, but I couldn't suppress my condescending grin. Henry seemed to ignore my expression, but he happily responded.

"Mark, those two are not mutually exclusive."

I caught myself before diving headlong into a debate about the "divine inspiration of Scripture" as Henry would defend it. This was not the setting for that, nor did I have the energy for such frivolous discussions. I stood silent for a moment, as if considering his words. But then, something he said rebounded to the forefront of my mind, and its implications offended me to the point of an unavoidable rebuttal.

"What does <u>He</u> mean when <u>He</u> tells you to trust in <u>His</u> timing? Were their deaths just a step in the grand chess game of eternity? Were their lives of such little value? Did God make you some sort of enduring protagonist, to remain standing while other people around you drop dead?"

Henry frowned through his bushy mustache.

"Mark, if I thought myself the main character in life, perhaps I would be seeing people as pawns on a chess board awaiting their turn to be taken. However, if I believe that God is the main character and I am just a detail, no better than anyone else, I can resign myself to a plan that is much bigger than I."

"So, does that leave you without consequence for your actions? Why worry about 'obedience' or 'sinfulness' if everything is subject to His will? Why try? Why care?"

Now, Henry's frown had crept into another one of those annoyingly peaceable smiles.

"We still have responsibility, Mark. We are made with a purpose."

"To die?" I spat in annoyance.

"I'll tell you what, Mark. Come to church with me this Sunday. We can sit in the very back, so that no one sees you."

"N—"

Before I could finish my rejection of his offer, he continued.

"I want you to keep challenging me with these questions. Come listen to the sermon. Write down whatever notes, oppositions, complaints you have. Then we can talk about it. It will be good for both of us, I think."

It felt like a trap.

"Henry, I grew up listening to sermons. I don't want to hear anyone else preaching at me."

"I understand, but you're a different person now. You've experienced a lot since you left the church. I've got a feeling that you haven't quite found all the answers to your questions."

"Oh, and I'm supposed to find them in a pew on Sunday morning?"

"Maybe... or maybe not. Someone of your —How did you phrase it once? Ah, yes— 'acuity' should be able to withstand one sermon while keeping your agnosticism intact."

"Atheism," I corrected.

"Still?" Henry raised his eyebrows in surprise. "Hmm", he tilted his head, as if weighing the feasibility of my claim. "We'll see."

That felt like a challenge to the integrity of my belief system. Before I was aware of what happened, I had somehow agreed to attend and even repeated back to him the time the service started.

He began rolling up his window, beaming with delight.

"See ya, bud!" he shot out, right before the window closed.

I swore, turning away. Somehow, he'd played me into going to church with him.

"Oh well, I can cancel anytime..." I reasoned with myself as I walked to my car.

Reaching for the door handle, I paused. Taking a glance in Henry's direction, I could see him already flitting through the manilla file again.

But if I back out, then I'm proving to him that I'm not confident in my assertions... No! I need to go, hear this message and prove to Henry and perhaps myself that there is no power in that book, no weight to its words, nor any imagined deity from whence it was derived. I will stride out of that church victorious; at last assured that I will no longer be troubled by Henry's religious beckoning. He will see how unfazed I am, and perhaps he will himself doubt the efficacy of his precious "gospel".

I climbed into my car wearing my own peaceable grin and

began to back out of the parking space. It was time to go get a fresh cup of French-pressed coffee and decompress with some light reading before my afternoon shift at the *Bale*. Perhaps for a change, the quaint reports on a small town's activities might give a feeling of respite. I felt as though I was about due one.

Henry had clearly defined what was permitted to be reported about the case. Despite my tenacity to excel and prove my worth as a journalist, I desired to honor Henry's request. Especially considering that the two victims were Henry's friends.

I pressed the brake at this thought. I was diagonally positioned across the middle of the parking lot. My eyes flicked to Henry, who was staring wide-eyed at his steering wheel. I knew then that something was wrong.

Without any hesitation, I returned to my parking space and got out, making my way to Henry's car. I stood again at the window for several moments before he opened it without looking up.

"Isaac didn't die of cardiac arrest."

"Who? What?" I asked, trying to pinpoint what he was talking about.

"Chief Knox... he didn't die of natural causes. He was poisoned!"

Correction... all *three* of the victims were Henry's friends.

I went rigid. The targeting of the unfortunate deceased was beginning to have a discernable commonality. My eyes fell on a stunned Henry.

A new chill crept up my spine and I, myself, began to shudder, inundated with an overwhelming sense of my own life being in jeopardy.

Misty's Letter to Henry – 27th of June 2023

Henry,

I do appreciate the sweet love letter that you wrote me, even though I feel it entirely permissible that you hold off this classical style of correspondence for now. The case of this Hunter gives me an anxiety that I haven't felt since Id was here.

Honestly, Henry, I am quite convinced that this Hunter is himself another demon, or at least another wicked person possessed by a demon...

Why us? Why Allison!?

I'm sorry, I know you have these questions too, and I'm simply asking out of anxiety. I just... have these nagging feelings.

After what you told me about Isaac...

At first, what seemed like an isolated, hateful crime seems to pulsate faintly to a pattern, like a dim indicator light.

One city council member killed in his pharmacy could seem like a random murder. Two members though, at separate times and locations; that hints at premeditation.

Jenny's death does confound this theory, though. The sweet girl was not on the council, so why did she have to die? I'm sorry, this question probably upsets you terribly. My dealings with the council make it a painful question for me too. Even though I only sat for one vote as a stand-in, I still care about each of the members. I've spent plenty of time around them at the mayor's office.

Why would someone attack our council anyway? It's not like they make major political or economic decisions for the world at large. I mean, their last meeting was completely absorbed in the decision about a new mural for the wall along the back of the 100-block of Main Street. Not exactly weighty stuff...

Regardless, I called and talked to Kelly for a while. Adam is having... a difficult time. You should give him a call when you have a chance. From the way Kelly made it sound, the whole family is paralyzed with dread, in light of the killings. She shares my sentiments about the Hunter's supernatural characteristics.

LEVI ARMSTRONG

Considering the eventful autumn that the Clemmenses just had, I don't blame them for locking down. The good news is Lia has quite the penchant for baking. She and I plan to stop by and deliver a warm meal and cookies to the Clemmenses in just a little while. Maybe that will cheer them and remind them that there are people nearby who love them... a whole church full!

I've enjoyed getting to know Lia more. She's a very sincere and genuine woman. I feel like she's the type of person you don't have to guard yourself around. Nor does she act guarded. She's one of those peaceful people, and it does the soul good to have a friend like her.

Speaking of our friends... how on earth did you convince Mark to come to church with us this Sunday? I'm stunned that he actually accepted your invitation.

I hate to say it, but he's probably got some ulterior motive. He's probably going to use sermon quotes in such a way that he can twist them for his next blog treatise on why the Church is toxic, or how religion is an enslavement of the mind... I'm sorry, that's not fair. I love Mark, and he's not as antagonistic as he used to be, but his constant need to prove his superior intellect rubs me the wrong way sometimes.

All the same, I will try to treat him lovingly and pray that both he and I will come to be better friends.

Oh, Henry, I do adore you. Don't think that since I spent this entire letter either hypothesizing or catastrophizing that I don't appreciate you.

I love you, Henry Paul Loadwain. Come home safe to me tonight.

Forever yours,
Misty

84

Prayer Journal of Kelly Clemmens – Night of June 27th, 2023

Oh God, my God,

I need your help! Something is very wrong. It feels as though our house has been infested by an unseen plague. I need You, God. I can't face this realm of darkness without You!

Misty and Lia came by this morning and in their overwhelming kindness, brought chicken poppyseed casserole and some incredible oatmeal chocolate chip cookies! They insisted on not coming in so as not to impose, but I really would have appreciated the company. Instead, they turned to leave and simply said that they missed seeing us at church.

It does tug at my heart to think about how we've been absent from church for the entire winter and spring. Adam has just become so paranoid. At first, I agreed that we needed some space from everybody following all the traumatic events that took place. Especially since I was in the throes of the first trimester back in the late fall, I was content with watching the live-stream of the church service. But as time went on, I stopped feeling the urge to go. And I know that if I'm being honest with myself saying that it's an inconvenience to meet in the library is just an excuse. I brought it up with Adam on two different occasions before today. On those two occasions, he seemed hesitant to return.

Seclusion, is a pretty spring to visit and refresh yourself in, but if you linger there too long, you'll get sick from the excessive consumption of mineral deposits in the water you drink...

Maybe that makes more sense in my head, Lord. I'm not a poet, like the Psalmists. Thankfully, my salvation doesn't depend on my writing ability!

What really troubles me, Lord, is not the past few months, my ineloquence or the fact that I'm a massive, pregnant beachball right about now. What really troubles me is Adam. He's acting very strange. As we commune right now, he's outside Merrin's window, measuring the dimensions so that he can board it shut. When I asked him what he was doing, he shook his head and said, "No more visitors."

"What?" I asked.

"They aren't allowed back."

"Who?"

"Those women."

"Misty and Lia? Why?"

"We can't allow anyone else in our home."

I was so taken aback, then I thought about the other night when he told me about the man at the door. It all seemed to make sense at last.

"Adam, these aren't strangers at the door, it's Misty!"

"But what about this 'Lia? What do you really know about her?"

"Well, Misty trusts her, and I trust Misty with my life."

"Yeah, and Henry trusted Mark Spasmen, and that turned out so well for us, didn't it?"

"But you know full well that it wasn't really—"

He cut off my protestation.

"The truth is that we can't trust any of them."

"Adam, that's abs—"

"No. More. Visitors."

His voice was so icy-cold that I almost felt... I can't believe I'm even saying this, but I almost felt like he was... he was threatening me. I fell silent, and evidently feeling like he had won, he climbed back up the ladder to the casement and started securing boards to seal off Merrin's window.

Lord, I don't know what's going on, but I know that I need to stay close to You in prayer.

Marcus Spasmen's Critical Analysis of the Christian Religion, as Displayed at First Baptist Church of Allison – July 2nd, 2023

Despite the congregation of FBC Allison meeting in the library today, given the ongoing reconstruction of the church itself, the attendants bustled about, apparently adapting to the new norm. There was an incongruous tumult of greetings and polite inquiries as one person asked another about how they and their family were faring. The seemingly pleasant inflections converged into a monotonous tone to me, absent of any real significance. I sat implacable, striving to be undisturbed and unnoticed.

To my chagrin, I was greeted by my old Sunday School teacher from when I was a boy. I couldn't recall his name for the life of me, but I knew his face. He seemed to have trouble recalling mine as well. As the painstaking conversation went on, I kept vacillating between attributing his loss of my name to apathy, or commonplace geriatric deterioration of recollective functioning.

He nodded so excessively. As if he too was ready to affirm me in what way he could and then return to the safety of his seat. I too wished for the stale conversation to end, but I was already retreated to my seat, and thus I was trapped; pinned down by social obligation to suffer this old man till he departed. The old man was just starting to apologize for the third time about my inability to visit the church at its building as it had been for the past seventy-five years when a familiar vice grip seized my shoulder. The old man's eyes lit up as he recognized the owner of the hand to be Henry.

"Well, Henry!" The old man, exclaimed.

"Mr. George, how are ya?" Henry asked, seemingly comfortable to endure the head bobs and breathy pauses between every three words.

"Fine. Just *breath* fine." Bobble-heading and raising a knobby and crooked finger to indicate me, he continued. "I was just *breath* getting to know *breath* this young man *breath* uh… Marcus?"

He looked at me with eyebrows raised to ensure that he had got it right.

I gave a brief smirk and nod. After pulling out a white handkerchief with a cursive "G" embroidered on it and coughing feebly, the old man furthered his explanation. All the while, Henry waited patiently for Mr. George's recovery.

"He's visiting *breath* with us *breath* for the first *breath* time today."

He let off, head bobbing and smile placidly aimed at Henry and I.

"Mr. George, this is Marcus Spasmen. Bryce and Cindy's son. He and I used to be in your third grade class. It was a looong time ago." Henry gestured with a hand going back over his shoulder, as if to indicate that time had passed behind his back.

That wrinkled smile widened, and a discernable twinkle glistened in his slightly fogged eyes.

"Mark Spasmen? *breath* Well, God bless *breath* you young man. *breath* You and Henry *breath* were only boys *breath* full of energy *breath* and questions."

The embroidered cloth returned to his mouth to receive another cough, then he painstakingly continued.

"Especially you, Mark *breath* I hope God *breath* has answered your questions. *breath*"

I thought that if I expounded upon my "apostasy", the disappointment might kill the man, so I sufficed to say, "Well, I seem to find myself lacking in that energy but abounding in questions."

The old man's smile only widened. "Well, good."

I assumed that Mr. George had checked out of the conversation and quite possibly forgotten who I was again, but then he continued, "That's good *breath* that just gives you *breath* more chances to see *breath* God at work."

I gave the man a genial smile, but I was doing my best to restrain my tongue.

"Mr. George, how is—" Henry's inquiry was cut off by a voice that resounded from the speakers affixed on collapsable stands that stood on each side of the congregation.

A heavy set, middle-aged man was wrapping thick fingers around a small aluminum music stand that served as a podium. I presumed this to be the David Kent that I had heard Henry and Grigory go on about.

"Good morning" the booming voice repeated. "We are glad that y'all are here today at First Baptist, Allison. I'm encouraged to see many familiar faces and a few new ones too." David said with a flit of his eyes toward me.

With that remark, at least half a dozen old women throughout the crowd rather conspicuously stole glances my direction. Subtlety is lost on the aged.

Being painfully aware of my observance, I missed a few of the following words that David spoke but tuned back in at the words "but first, I'm gonna ask brother Henry to pray before we sing."

Henry stood up from the folding chair next to mine and made his way to the pop-up platform. David stepped aside, and Henry wrapped his calloused, meaty hands around the edge of the "podium".

"Morning!" Henry said in his comfortable, southern boy air. His smile dwindled and he quietly said, "let's pray."

The room was silent for a few moments as everyone around me bowed their heads. I tilted mine but kept my eyes open. I, myself, was not praying (to be clear), but observing. As all their eyes closed, I began surveying from my peripherals. A child on my left, across the middle aisle was attempting to steal her mother's attention by playing peekaboo. The mother did her best to keep her eyes closed and ignore the girl, but had to occasionally reach a hand to lower the child's and give a silent shake of her head, mouthing, "no".

At last, Henry began praying. I thought that he had been trying to build up for dramatic effect, but when he finally spoke it was not bold or boisterous; it was something entirely different than what I expected. It was subdued, it was weak sounding, fragile even. The way he prayed was in stark contrast to the discipline and commanding presence that Henry typically elicited. I've done my best to recount the following prayer verbatim.

"God, You are good. Despite our pain and loss, You are good. Despite our weakness and inconsistency, You are good. Despite our doubt and sinfulness, You are good."

Henry paused, taking in a sharp breath before continuing.

"Father, I've seen You do incredible things. I've seen and felt glimpses of Your glory pierce the world around me. But still, I doubt You!"

I gaped at this admittance, I whipped my head about, scanning the room for pitchforks and torches, but instead, I saw tear-streamed cheeks, glistening against the lights on the ceiling. Heads were bowed but nodding in unspoken agreement. This scene confounded me. Were all these Christians admitting to themselves, at least, that they had doubts? Henry was the only one bold enough to confess that before everyone. Apparently, everyone was closer to apostasy than they let on.

Just then, a deafening sniffle came from the speakers.

"My God, You've... You've saved my wretched, undeserving soul, but still I fail You, all the time."

Even more than this incendiary admittance, I was taken aback by hearing Henry cry. I don't know if I've ever heard the man cry. A hero, a titan among men, gushing in front of a library full of people. Again, I scanned the room for judgmental looks, but all were seemingly ok with this scandalous scene. More than that, many seemed to place themselves in this defaming posture. Was church always like this and I somehow forgot? Surely not!

"How desperately we need You, Lord."

Henry sniffled again, and strangely, I felt a lump in my throat. It must have been sympathy for a friend so close.

"Solus Christus" Henry said reverently.

Since when did Henry speak Latin?

"In Your good name, amen."

Henry stepped off the stage without lifting his head. The music minister wiped his eyes as he approached the keyboard.

"Amen, amen." The minister said into a small wireless mic that had a thin cord running back behind his ear.

Henry sat down again beside me, still sniffing and wiping reddened eyes. I tried to feign not noticing, for the sake of his dignity.

The music minister asked us to stand up and sing whilst the keyboard began to play a familiar tune that slunk up from the recesses of my recollection. Archived lyrics sprung to the front of my mind as the tune continued, but I did not sing. How could I? Despite my attempts to maintain decorum, I could not emit words that I did not believe.

Apparently, these... hypocrites had found themselves at peace, admitting disbelief and still singing these songs that claim love, faith, and/or devotion. It pains me to consider that all the people in this room are hypocrites. Surely, they are simply so used to lying to themselves that the incongruency no longer flags as a disturbance in their mind. But I know for certain that Henry is too self-aware for permitting this incongruency. I also know that Henry is no hypocrite.

What could this mean? How does Henry believe, but not believe at the same time? How does he love this "God", but remain unable to be empirically certain that the deity exists? I fear that despite his best intentions, my friend has endured too much trauma to see things as they ought to be. I'm willing to defend Henry's character, but I can be contented to call the rest of those present "hypocrites".

The second song began, and the minister had yet to have reached the second verse before I noticed a tear trickling down Henry's face. Turning, I realized that he had several more tears leaking from his face. I nearly swore in incredulity but obviously kept myself composed.

"What is going on?", I thought. I nearly jumped out of my skin as someone interrupted my gawking by giving me a hug from behind. I knew the arms, and I immediately recognized the smell. Oh, how I dreaded explaining myself after the service. Despite the instantaneous inundation of anxiety, I put on a smile and turned to give my father and mother a proper hug. They were grinning from ear to ear to see me there. I felt bitterness seeping through my heart, as I knew that my intentions were only a greater disappointment to them. I would have to simply play this off as a "kindly visit", per the request of Henry. Frankly, I could have told them the truth, that I was actually there to pick apart the church from within, but they were probably thrilled just to see me.

My mind raced as the third song continued and I then had to listen to my father's nasal, off-key voice singing with no inhibition. Thankfully, the music ended after the third song. Dad grabbed my shoulders and gave them an affectionate squeeze as everyone moved to sit down. Pastor Kent returned to the podium and began his sermon.

My following notes on the sermon are based off the bullet points he provided, in addition to any Bible references he included. I've added a few interpretations and notes throughout but I tried to refrain from heavily critiquing in my notes. I hope to revisit these points and compare them to other interpretations of this segment of the book. Perhaps I will be able to capitalize on the inconsistency in how people understand the source, thereby giving proof to its fallacy. Admittedly, I will have to come to understand the original context of that segment, strictly in the historical sense. However, the passage preached has only the loosest association with anything historical beyond the book's first intended audience.

Revelation (Chapter 12: Verses 1 through 6)

1. The earth has shaken, thousands have died. Now a great sign is displayed in Heaven.
   - The pastor has indicated that previous chapters of the text describe several disasters befallen the country. I'd like to note that he made allusions to modern conflicts and natural disasters being signs

of these cataclysms beginning their rise. I do not think it is reasonably comparable to attribute the earth's natural climactic and tectonic processes to any supernatural phenomenon.

- "A woman clothed with the sun, with the moon under her feet, and on her head a crown of twelve stars."

  - I don't think I can provide any tangible interpretation of this excerpt beyond the most generous poetic interpretation. The pastor himself admitted that the woman would not have the sun wrapped about her, nor the moon supplanted to the soles of her feet, nor stars be adorning her head. In no capacity could this be physically possible.
  - Pastor Kent then implies that this pregnant woman is a representation of the nation of Israel. He says that the twelve stars around her head represent Israel's twelve divisions, also known as tribes.

- She was pregnant, about to give birth (v.2).

  - No explanation provided by whom she was impregnated. If the entirety of her character is symbolic, who or what does she represent? What then would her obstetric state imply?
  - Pastor Kent stated that the "most clear representation" of the expected child is actually symbolic of Jesus Christ.
  - So, I always perceived the book of Revelation as the paramount religious foretelling of eschatology, but this pastor indicates that the narrative easily switches between what "has happened" and what "will happen".

- I find his assertions presumptuous; given that he bases further interpretation on unfounded "past" events.

2. Another Sign in Heaven: A Great Red Dragon (much more interesting!)

- The dragon has seven heads, ten horns, and a crown on each head.
  - As any literate person could safely assume, this dragon represents the Devil. Although, the significance of the quantity of his heads and horns is not clear, it further supports the strange fascination religions have with certain numbers (three, seven, ten, twelve... etc.)

- The dragon's tail sweeps down a third of the stars.
  - Again, not a literal description (I hope).
  - Pastor Kent referenced another place in the Bible where it describes Satan causing a third of the angels of Heaven to fall with him, when he betrayed God. The pastor identified these fallen angels as demons. So... Henry's "Id" would supposably have been a traitorous angel, formerly residing in Heaven.

- The dragon intended to devour the child as it was born.
  - This is kind of a grotesque image presented in the text, but playing on Kent's supposed symbolism, it would indicate the Devil's hostility to the soon to be "Messiah".

3. Delivery and Departure (verses 5&6)

- The pregnant woman gives birth to the child. ("One who is to rule all the nations with a rod of iron...")
  - As my dearly departed friend, Jonathan, once expressed to me; everything in their

Bible does point to Jesus. The fixation on a figure whose existence is rather loosely verified goes to show the instability of the religion. If they can't prove all these miracles, then they try to base much of their philosophy and dogmatics around the life and teaching of one historical character. With that obsession comes the embellishment of his accounts.

- The child is "caught up to God and His throne."
  - The reverend correlates this image with Jesus ascending to Heaven, following his execution and "resurrection" where he was "reportedly" seen amongst his followers.
- The mother flees to the wilderness, where God nourishes her for 1260 days.
  - In following the symbolism previously mentioned, Pastor Kent arrives at the deliverance of the Jewish people; escaping the Devil's work. They bide their time that lasts for three and a half years.

Personal Review:

My conclusory review of the sermon omits the application points presented, due to their excessively sanctimonious tone. I found it hard to see how I was to apply anything -not that I intended to- from a list of metaphysical actions like: "Thank God for the fact that Jesus was the plan from the beginning to the end", or "Live, trusting that God will continue to provide", and so forth. I find these application points irksome and leading. One point I found particularly out of place was, "Remember that before the beast comes, the Church will be divided, and the wheat and chaff will be sifted. Now is the time to make sure that you are truly amongst the wheat!"

Overall, I would like to compliment Pastor Kent on the

research he put into his sermon, but for me, it is a mere fantasy story with a reservoir of well-developed lore. The pastor is akin to a scholar whose sole purpose is to broaden our understanding of the implications to be gleaned from a novel.

I imagine for someone like Henry, who believes that he has found himself on the verge of an eschatological occurrence, this sermon was somehow insightful, maybe even an "afflatus" of what he needs do.

I can't deny that the ideas of fallen angels and the end of days does seem like a tempting resolution to my concerns about the bizarre experience at Simm's drug store and the roaming meadow. However, there is no way that I can rationally land here (in the Bible) as the obvious solution for my existential questions. Perhaps, I can no longer deny that supernatural events do take place, and that there are beings beyond mere humans roaming about. But I'll be damned before falling prey to the dogmatics established by these convocations of zealots. The truth of the "Hunter" is out there, but I can't find it in this church!

The Fourth Hunt

Tonight, I strike the king of the beasts! Only a fool would go directly into the midst of the pride, especially if they knew how to retaliate. My frame has limits and even beyond the flesh I must concede at the Threat's command.

No, despite my inherent strength I will kill from the shadows. When I have claimed my trophy then I will use it to strike terror amongst the pride.

Under the cover of darkness, my oldest friend, I approached the lion's den. I could see glowing eyes, bespeckling the curtails of the sky. The eyes of the lions and lionesses surveyed while their chieftain slept. The den was affixed in a large clearing, backed up to a motionless pond. These cats had exclusive privilege to the watering hole.

A new moon shrouded me in darkness. The stars were faint and no other lights shone about the den. Soon, I would set the night ablaze.

I approached beneath the canopy of four clustered trees. Arriving at this concealment, I spotted a pair of lions walking together in silence. These lions were young, not fully grown into their manes yet. I could see the faint outline of their heads scanning about, at least, they were feigning vigilance, for neither spotted my skulking.

I sat still for several minutes, observing the cyclical nature of their patrols. These two returned from whence they came after approximately two minutes of patrol. After they crossed in front of my cover again, they would walk another thirty feet or so then diverge. One would turn left toward the bushes in front of the den. The other would turn right, to survey the perimeter of their home before turning back to rejoin his fraternal ally. This outlier would be my first kill of the night.

If he missed his rendezvous, the other cat would quickly assume suspicion. Therefore, I moved swiftly from slitting the first throat to position myself within the bushes along the second cat's return.

It was at the precise moment that lion number two raised

his head in curiosity that I took full advantage of that opening. With a swift lunge, my arm shot out from the shrub and sizzling blood watered the lawn. I moved both bodies into the cover of the bushes, then fixed my eyes on the now unguarded side of the den.

Like a wraith, I flew to the closest cave opening. I turned in the first cleft of the giant structure of stacked rock, filled with intricate tunnels and more space than any of these loathsome creatures could need. I advanced in the dark tunnel, at ease in the shadow, but still, I could feel that I was not alone.

My pace slowed as I came to a juncture. I heard a low growl, followed by a sharp inhale. The orange glow from my knife was the only light, and it seemed more than enough. Taking a poised step back, I evaded a deadly stroke. After the claw passed in front of my face, I leaned back in and slashed the outstretched limb, watching it fall limp as I severed clean through the extending muscles.

The lion proved to be a lioness, judging by her cry. That cry did not last long though. Once I hacked into the offending limb, I wrapped around the beast's side and punched my glowing blade into her lungs. The sound of grilling flesh outdid her dying whimper. Her initial outburst had carried all the way to the ears of other members of the pride. By the time I lowered her body to the stone, I could hear footfall padding in my direction.

In an instant, I kicked off from the rock on my left and pushed up onto a cutout several feet above the height of the encroaching enemies. Three lions, to be exact.

The first to arrive knelt to study the fallen lioness. The other two surveyed in both directions that their intruder could have gone. I loomed for a moment, considering which target to take first. With a silent inhale, I plunged down.

My impact crumpled the lion beneath me, pressing his face into the ground. I dove forward and sunk my dagger into the other kneeling lion's neck. As I lifted my legs from the crumpled one's neck, he forced out a groan. The sound drew the attention of my third enemy. He turned about in time to see me pulling my dagger out of the noisy, supine cat's back.

Irate, this final combatant lunged as I side stepped over the corpses and narrowly missed another slashing. He followed up, chasing my evasion with a second swing. I nicked his leg with a flick of my blade. The enraged beast roared as the pain sent him charging in a frenzy. He leapt, overshadowing me with his greater frame. As I fell back, I thrust my blade out just before we both crashed into the stone wall.

A cacophony of visceral fluids boiling and dying moans told me that the cat had just expired. These kills were indeed thrilling, but they weren't the pelt I was seeking. I knew that my true prey was nearby, so I withdrew my weapon from the latest foe and flicked away the bile before advancing deeper into the lion's den.

I glided through the tunnels with ecstasy. Blood-drunk, I didn't even waste time stopping to brawl the rest of the guardians. My arm simply whipped to the sides while I sprinted ahead, passing the blade through neck after neck. So many arteries severed, such delicious carnage. My skin crawled with euphoria, bathing in the viscous red.

This was my purpose. I am the arbiter of the final war. I am judgment, at last, wrought to the earth.

My eyes caught sight of the cave's last hiding place. I had reached my prize. At will, the fiery blade in my hand burst into a torch of blazing white flame. My smile was irrepressible as the blood of those already condemned ran down my face and into my mouth. I drank of their suffering.

Approaching the final chamber, I slid the razor-edged torch along the stone wall, sending sparks and bouts of flame everywhere, igniting the passage behind me.

The once bold king of beasts cowered against the far wall as I approached, drenched in the life-force of his pride. I was silhouetted by a heightening wall of flame, grinning as I brought damnation in my wake.

My dagger was poised for the night's final kill. With an abysmal growl of my own, I whispered through reddened teeth.

"I am the blood-warden of Hell."

Private Journal of Grigory Yakor – 2 July 2023

I'd like to think that despite having only four years under my belt in the fire service, I've managed to accumulate considerable experience in the job. Especially through the time of Id's oppression. I felt like I could easily say that I'd seen it all. Tonight, I learned just how wrong I was.

The day started off with our annual hose testing, which involved a lot of unloading and reloading of hundreds and hundreds of feet of attack and supply lines. The tedium came when the lines were charged full of water, with the nozzles closed and the pressure turned up to the desired PSI, but then we saw glistening little arcs of water escaping pinholes through random sections of hose. Any time a fifty-foot section of attack or supply line leaked, we had to halt operations, replace that section of hose, then restart the test timer. The same rule applied to the hundred-foot sections of large diameter hose (LDH), and those are significantly heavier (especially when full of water). Reloading that LDH was a chore that nobody wanted to do, so naturally, I found myself doing it. I don't say all this to complain, but just to give a description of the exhaustion that preceded the insanity.

Despite the fatigue from the extra work, I found a little bit of solace in the labor. There's something simple about keeping your head down and trudging on, fixated on the immediate need, trusting that your piece of a collective effort will bring about the desired result. This had been my approach to the fire scene: nose to the grindstone, don't look up, just keep moving. The problem with keeping your head down and your eyes fixed at what's right in front of you is that you're bound to neglect something significant in your surroundings. After tonight, I won't make that mistake again.

The afternoon was spotted with medical calls, so we didn't have a chance to catch our breath after hose testing. We decided that it was best to pick up pizza for supper instead of risking an interrupted attempt at cooking at the station. I sat in the back and breathed in that freshly baked pizza smell. I could feel my stomach shrinking with each oregano-scented whiff! I all but jumped out of the truck and carried our two boxes of pizza inside. The objective: no leftovers.

Cody, who hadn't been obliged to do anything besides run the pump during hose testing (given that he's been on light duty since coming back to work) was on the fringes of being hangry. I was relying on the Holy Spirit to keep me from showing how far down into "hanger" I was.

"Grab us some plates, would you, Grig?" Gandrix asked. I moved to obey. Then, the tones dropped.

†

With lips pressed tightly together, I awaited the designation of whose call it was.

"Westside"... of course. Chairs shifted, scuffing the floor behind me.

"10-70 Structure fire."

I spun and made for the door to the bay. Four-letter curses flew about behind me.

Turned out and ready to party, I pulled up the address on my phone while riding in the back of the truck. It appeared to be a solitary residence, tucked in the northwest corner of town. I could see on the map that a private pond and an extensive driveway surrounded a massive home.

"Hey Cap, whose house is this?" I asked while strapping on my air pack.

Captain Gandrix zoomed in on the mounted tablet in front of his seat. He studied it for a moment or two, then I saw his jaw drop.

His reply was another four-letter curse. We approached a secluded corridor of trees. I could swear that in the distance, a faint glow of orange hazed above the woods. Cody began to slow the firetruck. I leaned to the side and saw an ornate metal gate that stood about ten feet tall. It remained shut at our approach, bearing a large "H" at the center.

"What the Hell are you doing??" Gandrix shouted. "Smash through it!"

The massive engine shuddered to life as I heard Cody's foot slam the gas pedal to the floor. I listened to the RPMs soar as the gate grew closer. In a blink, galvanized metal was flung everywhere. Over the roar of the engine and the wail of the sirens, the impact of the gate felt like a distant bump. Our twenty-two ton rig faintly jolted as we rolled on toward the mansion.

We rounded a fountain pool with an elegant looking statue in the epicenter and then saw the staggering, three-storied home billowing out with flames from the first and second floor windows. The fire seemed to be coming from the alpha and bravo sides, near the corner. Black smoke crept out from the eaves. I stretched the line, knelt at the door, put my mask on, hood over and repositioned my helmet. I looked to Gandrix, who came and knelt next to me. I glanced over his gear briefly, ensuring that his armor was "tight, and ready to fight."

I gave him a nod before clicking in my SCBA regulator. He had been inspecting my armor, as well, and returned the nod before also clicking in. I aimed the nozzle to the garden on my right and pulled the bell back to clear the line of any air. Once all the air was bled out of the hose, I gave Gandrix another nod, and he spartan kicked the front door in. I grabbed the doorknob to control the flow of air until Cap joined me on the line. When he indicated, I let the door swing back open, we grabbed the hose and charged ahead, right into the belly of the beast.

✝

We advanced into a left turn soon after entry. The first room on the left appeared to be a large parlor area, judging from the piano legs and elegant furniture feet that were visible beneath the rapidly descending smoke layer. All above that layer was black.

Together, Captain Gandrix and I pushed low and fast across the parlor. Cody had been feeding us line into the doorway. Since we arrived a minute or two ahead of the other engine company, Cody was multitasking between pumping and supporting ground operations. I felt relieved when I heard sirens get louder then stop, indicating that Engine 2 had arrived on scene.

I felt the workload of dragging the hose significantly lessen. The guys from Engine 2 were now helping Cody on the outside.

The black pall before us deepened to an overwhelming aura of oblivion. Even though I could feel the heat intensify, we braved further.

"Come on," I said through gritted teeth; hungry for a sign of the enemy. The hose caught. Our advance stopped. The thermal oppression grew.

"We need more slack!" Gandrix shouted over his shoulder.

I squinted my eyes in the pitch, arms keeping constant tension on the line so that I could force ahead as soon as slack came. Then I saw it; the orange circular hue, emanating in heightening wrath.

"I said 'more slack!' Gandrix roared.

A smirk crept on my face, invisible to all save for the glow in front of me.

"Hello beautiful." I whispered to the enemy who couldn't help but betray itself. Its ravenous hunger gave way to light. The slack came, and we shot forward with an eager lunge.

†

In short order, Gandrix and I had knocked down the bulk of the flame in the room beyond the parlor. I began spraying into resilient hot spots that were between the wall and the corner of the ceiling. I could hear Captain Gandrix advising Chief Billy Davidson over the radio that the fire was contained on the first floor, and that we were extinguishing residual pockets of flame. I was only able to hear parts of what Chief Davidson was saying between the deep thuds of water tearing into burnt sheetrock, but apparently Engine 2 was sending a pair of guys upstairs to attack the fire on the second floor.

Once I finished soaking down that corner of the ceiling, Gandrix gave a firm pat on my shoulder then gestured to the door on our right. The door opened into a long hallway that was littered with paintings on the right and tall windows on the left. The smoke layer was significantly diminished in that hallway, only lessening the further you went. I pulled the line toward its portal when Gandrix told me to wait while he checked with the thermal imaging camera. Nothing seemed significant enough to him. He advised me to grab a pike pole, then start tearing out some of the ceiling in that alpha-bravo corner room.

As the smoke had lessened since we contained the fire, I was able to walk back toward the entry hallway with some visibility. I caught a glimpse of the flashing red lights reflecting off the front door that hung ajar. I had nearly made it to the door when I felt a vaguely familiar sensation of cold. I grabbed the pike pole that had been set right outside the doorway, assuming that the sudden drop in temperature was due to our extinguishment operations.

I quickly made my way across the parlor when I caught a glimpse of somebody's shadow running back toward the entrance, around the far side of the grand piano. I whipped my head to follow them, but they were gone before I could track them.

"Uh... Cap?" I called, trying to understand what he was doing running about like that. A familiar anxiety seeped into the back of my mind, like moisture soaking through a towel.

"Yeah?" Captain Gandrix asked, from about ten feet in front of me, just inside the door to the corner room beyond the parlor.

I let out a sigh of relief. "I think one of the guys is freelancing. He just ran by me. Do you see anyone else?"

"Nope," he said carelessly, grabbing the pike pole and beginning to pierce holes into the sheetrock overhead. Gandrix was not one to wait around for work to be done by others. But he had told me to start tearing ceiling.

"Hey Cap, let me get that. You told me to do it, anyway."

"Sure, it don't matter to me." He handed me the pike pole, then picked up the nozzle.

I was glad to have another Captain who wasn't afraid to put in the labor, but how could I just stand there while my supervisor did the grunt work?

We carried on in this way till our low air bells had been ringing for a few minutes. Neither of us minded delaying the retreat a little longer. However, when I glanced at his integrated PASS device reading four-hundred psi, I grabbed his shoulder and said, "It's time we back out."

He looked up, satisfied with the work we had done. Laying the nozzle on the ground, we followed the path of the hose back out to the front door. When we exited the building, we saw that Cody had set up the rehab station off and to the right of the fountain.

Stewman, the driver/engineer for Engine 2, was helping Cody with the supply line. Thankfully, the architects of this mansion had the decency to ensure that a hydrant was within five hundred feet of the house. Freshly tested LDH was connected to the truck and bulging from the constant influx of water from said hydrant.

Cody came up and handed Gandrix and me water bottles from the cooler as I pulled my mask off my face. I savored the icy drip over my hands and even soaked my neck with the chilling beverage before finally guzzling the remaining contents in a single tip. Gandrix sat on my left and was also cooling his head and neck with his bottle before downing the rest.

"Good job, Cap." I said, extending a fist bump.

He nodded his head without saying anything, then requited my gesture. It was hard to get a read on him sometimes. Cody came up behind us and began unscrewing the empty air bottle on my back.

My eyes shifted in an instant from the captain's sweat-soaked face to another shadow that zipped across my view, a couple hundred feet away, just before the wood line. Captain Gandrix noticed my stiffening posture, and he craned his neck to see what had arrested my attention. The figure was already gone, having moved behind the mansion.

"What is it?" he asked.

I hadn't been able to see clearly who it was, but I thought

it looked like a civilian running around the house. That would prove a liability, but even an overly involved neighbor encroaching on the scene would be better than the dreadful alternative that gnawed at the back of my mind. But I didn't know how to share my real concern, so I just summarized in a way that would keep him engaged.

"I think someone is freelancing on the back side of the building. I just saw them run that way." I felt a new air bottle snap into place on my pack. I turned and gave Cody an appreciative nod. He simply patted me on the shoulder without a word. This gesture left me uncertain if he was actually mad at me for the last fire. Something we would have to discuss later.

Captain Gandrix rose to his feet with a groan and looked around, counting personnel: Cody, Chief, Stewman, and Officer Carlyle. Callahan and Captain Earnheart were on the inside fighting fire.

"Carlyle, any of your guys here, besides you?"

"No, not yet." The police officer (who was for some reason wearing civilian clothes) said absently, then added "I think one or two more are on the way." He gestured with his phone in his hand. He looked pale... even nervous. Why was he nervous? He wasn't fighting fire.

"Well..." Gandrix said slowly, unsure of what to think about my report.

We both turned to see the ambulance pull behind Engine 2, and the doors open.

"On time, as usual." Captain Gandrix said with his sweaty eyebrows raised. "Then who was that creeping around?"

I looked back toward the wood line, a cannonball of a sinking feeling deep down in my gut, but the longer we sat there, the bigger the cannonball got.

"Come on," Gandrix said.

I shot to my feet, ready to ease my suspicions, one way or another. I was certainly less anxious to check it out with the captain at my side. We advanced across the fire ground, making our way to the alpha bravo corner of the house. As we passed, I observed the damage dealt by the fire. Windowpanes had been blackened, and a section of stucco walls had nearly melted to the ground. I studied this destruction while walking.

"Grig?" A familiar voice called out.

I turned to see Henry, running up with Carlyle. They joined us as we rounded the house.

Henry continued to take in more of the scene as we four marched together.

"I can't believe it." Henry said. "Have they found anyone inside?"

"No, not yet." Gandrix answered.

"Hey Captain Gandrix," Carlyle came to a halt and grabbed the A-Shift captain on the arm. "What did you see that might be the possible cause?" Their voices trailed off as Henry and I rounded the Bravo/Charlie corner of the house.

We both stopped and stared for a moment. There was a sort of morbid beauty to the scene. Before us, laid an expansive veranda with a large round swimming pool at its center. Beyond the far parapet, was a serene pond, that looked to be nearly the size of a small lake. A tall flagpole stood erect, with the American Flag whipping about in the growing shadows. In the dying light, clouds were lofted in a gray line; thin and all but transparent. Beneath the natural clouds, a dense black force pushed its way upward, like an ambitious pillar into the sky beyond. The smoke, in its own dour way, somehow added to the picturesque scene.

"Well, this looked a lot different the last time I was here." We both kept our eyes on the landscape.

"You've been here before?" I asked surprised.

"Yeah, it's..." Henry cut off midsentence.

Both of us saw something move at the same time.

Out from the right side of the property a man was walking quickly, hunched forward, making his way around the far wood line, headed toward the Charlie/Delta corner of the house. It took me a few seconds, but I came to realize that I knew that person. Despite wearing the everyday civilian clothes, I recognized the stocky frame and mustached face to be that of

Captain Andrews, who was supposed to be home sick! He called out first thing this morning.

"Uh…" I paused, unsure of what to say. "Cap!?" I then called loudly.

He didn't respond but then disappeared behind the first structure. Beyond the veranda, beyond the pool. At the far extension of the house's rear was a large pool-house that joined to the main body of the mansion. In the farthest window stood another figure in front of what was evidently an open grill. The windows around him appeared to be the kind that swing wide, to allow plenty of ventilation for cooking. However, they were not open at the time. We squinted to watch close while advancing cautiously onto the veranda. The longer I looked at the person, distant in the shadows, the more I felt the hair on my neck straightening. Something was very wrong.

The figure moved suddenly, reached down and lofted what looked like a propane tank!

Henry grabbed my arm like a vice grip. The man in shadows raised his other hand and something began to glow orange. Something that looked like a knife!

Henry began to pull me away, but that wasn't going to be enough. The shadow moved his arm to slam the orange blade into the tank. We both turned to run. A loud and fast whistle rang out. I tackled Henry over a stone bench, then spread myself out across his body, covering his head with my own as the world shook!

I was pelted with chunks of stone, and I felt my ears burn overhead as flames whipped out across the sky, enveloping the veranda. Henry roared in pain. I tried to cover him more, but the side of his face was burned by the flames that whipped around me.

In a few seconds, the flames withdrew, and I looked about before removing myself from Henry. Some of the shrubs around us were burning like torches. The bench symmetrically opposed to ours, just outside the pool-house had evidently been blown to bits. I then understood why I was getting pelted with chunks of masonry. The roof had literally been blown off the pool-house, and flames now raged high across the back, Charlie/Delta corner of the mansion.

Far behind us, I heard Gandrix swearing aloud. I helped Henry to his feet, who was nursing his blistered cheek, doing his best not to swear.

"I said pull the damn horn!" the on-duty captain yelled into his lapel mic.

The long horn blast rang out, loud and clear. That was the signal for everyone to evacuate the mansion.

I turned to Henry, who stared at the slab where the pool-house once stood.

"Was that—?" I began to ask.

Henry turned to look at me. Neither one of us could find the words. There's no way. We saw him die.

A deep, painful wail rose from somewhere above us. We scanned around, then Henry cried out, "Look!"

I turned to see someone pressed up against the upper balcony parapet hiding beneath a blanket, shielding themselves from smoke and the flames on the nearby rooftop that licked toward them like a snake, sniffing out its prey. The huddled figure wailed again as we called out to them. The cry sounded weak, like that of an old woman; fatigued yet terrified. I radioed for a ladder to come to the back side of the mansion but got no response. The old woman screamed again, this time, more pained.

We both ran for the door entering the back of the house. Smoke pushed out and enveloped us when we entered. Henry and I immediately began coughing. I instinctively grabbed for my mask and regulator. Cinching my mask down, I took that initial breath that allowed clean air to start flowing my way. I thanked Cody again in my mind. Henry kept coughing.

"Wait outside, I'll be right back."

"Absolutely not." Henry said without hesitation. He then retched.

"Please, you can't breathe in here. Just make sure that we

come back out!" He looked at me with a furrowed brow. I thought I caught a twinge of anxiety in that stern face, but then he nodded and retreated to the dim light outside the door.

I advanced into the haze with a right-hand search. My hand on the wall, I knelt and slid and shuffled my way along, bumping into a leather chair and a lampstand that sat next to a built-in bookshelf. I maneuvered around the back of the chair and kept going. Through the thick gray smoke, I spotted a slanted rail up ahead of me. "Stairs", my heart leapt! "I might be able to save this one in time!" I told myself.

I slid toward the rail and then rammed my knee into something dense yet forgiving. My instincts told me what it was before my mind could even form the words.

"Henry, I've found someone!"

"What?" my friend called from somewhere across the sea of smoke.

"I've got somebody."

"Are they ok?"

I removed my fire glove and put my hand to the person's neck to palpate a carotid pulse. The ambient heat warmed my hand, like holding it inside an open oven. I reached for their neck and the skin gave way. I found my fingers swimming in the midst of wet, flat vessels. I withdrew my hand in disgust and examined my fingers.

"Blood." This person's throat was sliced wide open. "Dead", I called to Henry.

The old woman's cry rang out again. I could hear it from above me, up the stairs. I stuffed my hand back in my fire glove and reached for the railing of the staircase. Swinging around the bottom newel post, I began my vault up the steps. I hadn't made it three steps when I tripped and nearly toppled all the way back down to the first floor.

My foot had caught something. I looked on the steps in front of me and leaned closely, barely able to distinguish anything through the smoke that was turning from gray to black. When I finally got close enough, I saw that it was another body. Their legs had been sticking out across the steps. I felt my way to their head and leaned close to possibly see through the haze.

The middle-aged man's neck hung to his right from an unnatural angle, and a blackened splash of blood arrayed the wall next to them. He wore a simple black suit, the white dress shirt now soaked in blood. I felt that familiar chill traverse my spine again.

"I've got another one, Henry!" I called.

No response. I tried my radio. It wouldn't key up to allow me to talk. I looked at the screen, it blinked once then went blank. I admit that I swore at this point. (Lord, forgive me.)

"Please, somebody help!" The voice of the old woman cried from up above.

"Блин!" I said through gritted teeth, tucking my radio into its pocket, and climbing up over the corpse. I made sure not to trip over his legs this time. I reached the landing between floors then stopped, gaping as I knelt and saw two more corpses. One man, one woman. Each dressed in similar black suits. Both their necks had been split wide open, and the wall was stained in broiled blood.

I tried to swallow down my terror at finding four people dead within ten feet of each other. If that woman is still alive, the killer might be here as well, drawn to her obnoxious cries.

"Hurry! *Cough cough* It's *cough* getting hard to breathe!" she cried from somewhere to my left when I reached the top of the stairs. Instinctively, I crouched when I got to the second floor. The black smoke was thick, and I could see orange pulsing from somewhere far to my right.

I crawled my way toward the patio door, keeping my eyes fixed on the faint light from outside. I had nearly reached the door when I felt that same fleshy obstacle underneath my hand. This time, I found three lifeless masses, piled on top of one another, as if carelessly discarded. The floor around them was a lake of dark red blood, saturated into the carpet.

I didn't have time to stop. If these had been killed, the old woman was next! I could see her huddled figure there, pressed down against the parapet.

I burst through the door and was met with an explosive push of flame on my right. I staggered momentarily but recovered as the explosion receded.

"Are you hurt?" I called aloud, kneeling through the dense cloud of black. "I'm gonna get you out of here, ok?" My hand reached out to secure the woman. Instead, my hand hit stone where she once crouched. Squinting about, I tried to find her. Then, I dropped my hand to the floor of the balcony. It rested on another motionless body. My heart sank.

"Oh no." I breathed. "Ma'am!?" I shouted, reaching for her neck to feel a pulse. A strange sensation overwhelmed me as I extended my fingers to palpate for a pulse and there was no jaw line to rest against. There was no jaw. There wasn't even a head! I heard the woman's wail again, this time, it was all around me and I froze, paralyzed with fear. My eyes looked down again, realizing now that it was not a woman's headless body, but a man's. He lay there, in a bathrobe, with his head surgically removed, the edges of his neck appeared to have been burned as they were cut. As if the beheading was a precise cauterization. Despite the clean cut, it still allowed every ounce of blood in his body to leak out.

The old woman's voice resonated with a hysterical cry. The cry changed rhythm and became a sort of breathy hysterical laugh. It took every ounce of willpower I had, but I turned around to face the murderer, who I, at last, knew had been right behind me.

An elongated figure towered in front of me. His form phased in and out of visibility, blending in with the black smoke. I saw teeth gleam through the darkness. Sharp, wolf-like teeth.

My pulse pounded in my head. Memories of Id flooded my mind. I couldn't breathe for several seconds. This onyx being was taller than Id and skinnier, but somehow even more terrifying in how he loomed. He studied me, perfectly comfortable with the chaos about us. I couldn't make out what his eyes looked like through the heavy smoke, but I knew that he was studying me. His indiscernible gaze lasted another moment, then he silently raised his knife.

I say "knife", but it was nearly the length of a short sword. Regardless, I knew that I had seen the weapon before. Id wielded it, he killed thousands with it, parading throughout history, bending men to his will and slaughtering any who were an inconvenience.

Tonight, however, was the closest I had ever studied the weapon. It wasn't on fire at the time, but its charcoal-colored blade had what appeared to be veins of orangish-red pulsing up and down in lightning bolt patterns. The hilt was rounded like that of a Roman sword. The grip constantly glowed a deep red. A faint sizzling sound was emitting from the monster's weapon. Near the point of the knife, was a coating of blood, presumably from the dead man on the ground behind me.

The Hunter raised the weapon to his face, holding it symmetrically before him. Then he grinned his wolf-like grin; massive white fangs protruding from his lips.

I felt the urge to run, but I couldn't move. I was immobile, pinned by disbelief. I had thought that we were finally free from this evil.

The demon opened his mouth and a long, forked tongue wrapped around the blade. It began to sizzle loudly as the monster was evidently burning his own tongue! He licked clean all the blood that had soaked the tip of his weapon. I felt my legs begin to give way. Something clanged against the stone parapet behind me.

His tongue lifted from the tip of the blade with a distinct flicking sound, and in doing so, the knife ignited into a ripping spout of flame. On either side of the edged torch, two fiery orbs burst to life. I recognized those eyes! If any doubt had lingered that this was something besides another of Id's race, that doubt vanished then, and I faltered, admittedly terrified.

The demon's voice rumbled low and long.

"I am the Blood-Warden of Hell."

I staggered backwards as the monster whipped his blade

around.

"Oh Go—" my words cut off as I tripped back over the corpse of the headless man.

"What the—?" Henry's voice shouted out from behind me.

The suddenly flaming knife screeched across the air right in front of my face, slicing clean through the front brow of my fire helmet. I plowed backwards over the parapet, sending Henry, the ladder he just laid, and myself sprawling through the air, headed straight into the shrubbery on the side of the veranda.

"OOF!" Henry let out as he landed atop the dense, charred remains of a boxwood bush.

I gave a breathy "Ahhh", as I found myself face down in a particularly sharp holly thicket. Thank God that I was protected by my turnout gear. However, some of those singed, spiny leaves managed to find their way through my hood and under my jacket (I still took that as a win, considering the alternative). The ladder had flipped over the hedge and clanged its way into the pool.

Henry and I rolled off our shrubs and laid side by side on the ground. I painstakingly unstrapped my helmet, pulled back my hood and removed my mask. We both stared up at the balcony that was now completely engulfed in flames.

What could I say? So much just took place, but I just couldn't find the words to speak. We just stared up at the mesmerizing inferno lapping out into the evening sky.

"You think we should move back?" Henry asked with a breathy chuckle.

Just then, pieces of rock started falling around us.

"Yeah, ha-ha, good idea." I let out a whimsical laugh.

We made our way off the left side of the veranda, beyond the bench where we had taken refuge from the explosion. Night had fully set in, but this entire side of the house was ablaze, and the world around us was lit up like mid-day. I turned to look out over the pond and tried to steal a glimpse of beauty amid the insanity.

It was then that I finally noticed the ball positioned atop the flagpole. This ball was not like the typical, perfectly spherical adornment that nested atop other flagpoles. This, I came to realize wasn't even a ball. It was too oblong, too angular. This... was a human head.

A head, that I came to find, belonged to Mayor Haldent.

CHAPTER 5

I have no reason to stay up this late, but after what we saw tonight... how can I sleep? I imagine Grigory is having an equally tough time resting right now, even though we did steal a chance to unwind over some pipe tobacco on the back porch of the fire station. I know that I've got a lot of work to do in a few hours, when I should presumably be waking up, but I don't see myself getting much sleep anyway. Sometimes, I feel like it's just easier to throw up my hands and say, "I'll try that sleep thing again tomorrow night. I'll figure out how to do it, one of these days." I know that's probably not healthy, but if I had wanted the assurance of safely making it to old age with a clean bill of health, I wouldn't have joined the police department.

As it happened, after the encounter with this new demon (that we only know as "the Hunter"), I ensured that the firefighters maintained crime scene integrity throughout their playtime. Once the fire was out, and I was permitted to enter what was left of the structure, I took photos of the charred bodies. Grig reported at least eight bodies located within the mansion, including Mayor Haldent's. I can honestly say that tonight was the first time I've photographed a decapitated person's head as it sat on the tip of a flagpole.

What Grig didn't realize is that when his Fire Chief had walked around the right side of the property, he discovered two more bodies. He tripped over the first one when rounding a hedge. The second, he spotted and began CPR on but ultimately realized that the person was already as stiff as a board.

I, myself, wasn't aware that Mayor Haldent had his own personal security detail. It must have been a new development, because I don't recognize any of the other victims. I imagine that he went ahead and hired outside of the department because our numbers are so few now. Considering what just happened, I can hardly suppress the sense of relief that it's not Carlyle, Tommy, or Gamble, lying there with their throats torn out. Even though the loss of any life is still a tragedy, I'm only glad that it's not one of my guys.

Anyway, after loads of paperwork, and an incredibly irritating phone call with the feds, I finally clocked out. However, I didn't head straight to the house, as I mentioned before. I went by Grig's station and found him scrubbing fire hose outside the bay with a long brush. He waved and grinned when I pulled up into a nearby parking space.

I got out and walked over to the garden hose reel that he cleaned with.

"Well..." I started.

He chuckled and kept scrubbing down the length of the wide fire hose.

"Well..." he said, shaking his head and grinning.

I began to spray the section of the fire hose that he had already washed. We worked in silence for another minute or two as he finished scrubbing the last section of hose and I came behind him and rinsed away the soap suds.

"What are we going to do, Henry?"

He asked while gathering up the wet hose, soaking himself in the process, and moving it all to the inside of the bay.

"I mean, we know how to fight it, or... not fight it, really, but we still have to find the man that the Hunter has possessed, so that we can exorcise the demon within."

Grigory talking about exorcism felt so oversimplified.

"Well," Grig corrected himself as he laid out the last bit of hose like an accordion causing it to stand up on its edge, "We didn't really exorcise Id either, did we? We just got the crap kicked out of us while attempting to thwart his plan to kill the

Clemmenses and take over the entire world."

"Yes, just that." I said with a chuckle before Grig continued down his rabbit trail.

"We technically didn't even win the fight. God did. We happened to admit our inadequacy just in time, I guess."

Thinking back on my fight with Lionel, I remember expecting death at any moment, but somehow all of Lionel's —well Id's— assaults were near misses. The only lasting effect of the conflict is the scar on my stomach where he used that dagger to sling lava at me. It immediately burned through my clothes and ate away at my skin. The thought of that dagger in the hands of yet another servant of the devil sent a shiver up my spine.

Grig didn't seem to mind my silence when his train of thought concluded. After dusting his hands, he patted them on his soaking wet duty pants and nodded toward the firetruck. I followed him as he led me to the door of his seat. He climbed up inside the cab and stepped back out with his fire helmet in hand. He looked at it, whistled then handed the helmet to me.

I took it, confused by his gesture at first. Then, I looked down and saw what he was wanting to show me. The front bill (or whatever it's called) of his fire helmet had been chopped and melted, like someone took a scalpel and sheared off a perfectly straight section. The black shell of the helmet had bubbled and oozed, then cooled in a distorted wave-like pattern. I studied it for a few more moments.

I felt my heartbeat pick up pace. The thought that Grig was this close to being killed suddenly made me feel sick to my stomach. I can't handle losing him too. I'm done losing friends. We are going to stop this monster before anyone else dies!

I handed the helmet back to Grig. "Well thank God that you're a klutz, bud. If you hadn't stumbled back..." My joke fell off. I couldn't even broach the idea with a sarcastic cover.

"Yeah, ha, excellent work with the ladder, there, Henry! Highly effective!" Grig evidently wanted to help me recover from my dud joke, or he too was avoiding thinking about how he almost died.

I chuckled despite myself and found the energy to play along.

"Why thank you, I believe that with my help, you were able to descend the ladder in record time!"

He tossed the helmet back into the firetruck with a laugh and closed the door. "Well, descend *with* a ladder, at least. Ha-ha! Not sure whether it or I hit the ground first."

I just laughed and shook my head before nodding for him to come over to the patrol car. He followed me and waited while I fished in the console for my tobacco pipe. When I turned around and showed it to him, he grinned like a boy seeing a shiny toy. Without a word, he ran into the station and was back a minute later with his own pipe in hand. His pipe was not a basic corncob, like mine. His tobacco pipe was a long churchwarden with a curve to it. It looked like something an old philosopher from the late 1800's would be gripping in their self-portrait. I nodded with respect. We went over to the table out in the bay of the fire station.

"Let us discuss," I said as I sat down in an office chair with half its black leather finish worn off.

"Yes," Grig agreed. "We seem to premeditate our best demon-hunting while enjoying a little bit of pipe tobacco."

Grigory stuffed his pipe with some red cavendish.

I began while he first lit his pipe, "The problem is... this demon is more discreet, more precise than Id was."

Grigory coughed, after inhaling too sharply. "A mansion fire is discreet?"

"Well, I mean, if he reveals himself, he's only revealing his demonic form to us. The human that he's feeding on has remained hidden. He realizes that the man is his weak point, and he needs to guard it. Id paraded about that sanctuary as Lionel. His identity was only obscured by the bear hood and some smoke. At one point in the woods, he even lowered the head of the pelt and looked at me."

I lit my pipe and pulled the gentle flame in while letting Grig digest what I had just said.

"So, are we even sure that the Hunter has possessed a person, and isn't just materializing around Allison when he feels like killing somebody?" Grig filled his mouth with smoke, then he blew it out in a wisp and continued. "That's another thing. We don't even know why this demon is here killing people!"

"Could it be that dagger? Is that what drew the Hunter to Allison? And if so, what does he plan to do with it?"

I wasn't expecting Grigory to respond to my barrage of questions. I just shot them out as they came to mind.

"I am the Blood Warden of Hell." Grig said in a hushed voice, eyes fixedly peering through a cloud of smoke.

"What?" I asked, feeling unsettled at hearing Grig mutter those words.

"That's what he said to me right before we fell off the balcony."

"What does that even mean?"

"I haven't the foggiest."

"Now what does *that* mean?"

"Oh, come on, Henry! You've got to keep up with your British slang."

"But you're Russian!"

I glared at him, feeling annoyed that I couldn't escape the company of people who enjoyed wordplay. Mark is worse than Grig though, much worse. Jonathan isn't... Jonthan wasn't far behind Mark in using a broad vocabulary with five-dollar words. But here I am, and this guy who's only been in the US for the past seventeen years or so is running me over with his use of the English language in both American and British variations... Why me?

"It means 'I don't know.'"

"Yeah, I gathered that from context clues. I just hadn't heard it before."

Grig pursed his lips and made a "tsk, tsk, tsk" sound. He then winked. He's lucky that he was sitting across the table. I had half a mind to slug him.

I attempted a pull on the pipe, but we had been so busy jibing that I let the flame die. I reached for the box of matches and relit.

"There's nothing in the Bible that mentions this 'Blood-warden', is there?" I asked, fairly certain I knew the answer already.

"Not that I can think of." Grig replied, but he pulled out his phone to search, just to be safe.

I pulled contemplatively on my pipe for a moment while Grig searched on his phone for the answer.

"Nope," he finally said.

I steeped on that for a minute.

"The demons know Scripture, right?" I asked, leading Grig into my next thought.

"Huh?" Grig let out a puff of smoke. "Oh, yeah, I imagine they know it better than you or I. Think of when Satan tried to tempt Jesus in the wilderness, and he quoted the Old Testament to Him."

"Yeah, Satan just twisted the wording of Scripture for his own purpose." I began.

Grig nodded, his eyes broad, as he chewed on the implications.

"Well, who's to say that the demons wouldn't develop a rank and structure for their forces, in a manner and purpose outside of what we can read in the Bible. In fact, I would bet that they would prefer that."

Grig nodded again, this time a little faster.

"It would be awfully convenient if we knew exactly what the Hunter's step-by-step plan was, just by simply opening Scripture and reading it. We stumbled our way into finding Id's plan for dominion, but the Hunter hasn't created a single symbol. Can we assume that he's got some other purpose in mind?"

Grig finally stopped nodding and cut in. "So where do we start figuring out the Hunter's plan?"

I went to take another pull on the pipe, but I had done so much talking that the flame went out again. I dismissed the pipe by setting it on the table.

"We find the possessed man who is being used to facilitate these crimes. He is the path to follow. When Mark was possessed by Id, he managed to give us key information into Id's final steps before the brawl at the Site of Dominion. Hopefully, we can find the perp sooner than later."

Grigory tapped the ash from his pipe into a nearby ashtray.

"So, you have any suspects in mind?" Grig's accent came through a little heavy when he asked. Almost as if he was staging the question to answer it himself. I studied him as he cleaned his pipe. The slight frown he wore told me that he wasn't happy about his own answer to the question but was going to dutifully share it.

I gave a slow, purposeful nod. "I have... questions."

He responded in kind, "I do, too."

Marcus Spasmen's Personal Memoirs – July 2nd, 2023 (9:34 PM)

It's ironic that I always seem to find myself alone, making significant discoveries about these cases. Henry is nowhere to be found, off galivanting about in his patrol car, while I am simply stumbling over essential clues. I've already tried calling him, but he didn't answer. I plan to try again after concluding this entry, but best not risk forgetting any significant details in the time lapse.

I'm off from the *Bale* this evening, so I had every intention to spend my free time exploring Allison's library for some books on Agnosticism. After a goodly portion of preemptive research, I was delighted to find that a vast number of well-known scholars were astute enough to brave this pragmatic mode of spirituality. It seems there are countless others who have interacted with, or merely perceived the likelihood of something supernatural, but were bold enough to resist the magnetic pull from culturally established explanations of divinity. I admire this. I can no longer deny the supernatural, but I cannot accept organized religion. It's too convenient, too quick to sweep all the real ugliness under the rug. Yes, admittedly, I've seen some supernatural… things, but I've also seen the gnarled corruption of the world around me. There must be something at work that we can't see, but no "good God" would abide all the filth that has taken place throughout history.

All that being said, I appeased my scholastic appetites straight through dinnertime and until well after the sun went down. Thankfully, tonight was not "Word-Scramble night", so the senescent Miss Priverly had to endure my presence until normal closing time. I had my phone on silent and I wasn't wearing a watch, so I kept track of the time by observing the passive aggressive glances and repeated sweeping of the same section of floor around my chair. As the process began to repeat in closer succession, I knew that closing time drew near.

It's all because I told her that Jane Eyre was not a believable character. I didn't expect that my simple comment would be the stroke that severed any future dialogue with the woman. I mean, what's the point of literary analysis if you can't critique the work? How was I supposed to know that Miss Priverly was a Charlotte Bronte sycophant?

As I said, by the wordless communication from my archival nemesis, I knew that the time to depart had come. I stood up and approached the front desk with Caldwell's *Daring Not to Believe: Assertions without Certainty From Above.* After a rather delayed return to the desk, Miss Priverly read the title and flicked a glaring eye toward me before running the book under the scanner. With a victorious smile, I nodded my head and tucked the book under my arm. I rounded the column nearest the exit and stopped in my tracks to observe a small plaque that I'd never noticed before. The photo in the plaque held a crowd of people. At the center of that crowd was a small line of individuals standing apart. Each of them was holding their own book. One of the people in the forefront, the one that caught my eye was none other than Misty Loadwain. She stood there with the mayor, the late police chief, the late Joseph Simm, and someone that I know I've seen around town. There was a small inscription beneath the picture.

"To the heroes who saved our library."

It must have been the work of the Priverly woman. She fits the type to be melodramatic, and she surely has enough free time to design her own commemorative plaque. I snapped a picture of it to send to Henry and ask for more details, maybe even chide Misty for being a "hero". I sometimes appease myself by seeing how much I can irritate the poor girl.

Stepping out into the night, I felt an irrepressible warmth meet me like an ocean wave. I stood there, for a moment, trying to decide if the heat of the day had let off enough for it to be comfortable to spend more time outside, or would I find myself with a large circle of back sweat within five minutes? I heard the heavy click of the lock behind me and turned to see the librarian's bespectacled leer through the thick glass door.

I shook my head and chuckled. Then, in a moment of

spontaneity, I decided to pay a visit to an old acquaintance.

†

Admittedly, when I crossed the threshold of the cemetery gate, I began to feel a sense of anxiety creep into the back of my mind. I knew that there was nothing awaiting me in the cemetery at night, but I couldn't fight that slippery feeling of dread. I looked to my left at the scaffolds and exposed beams from the remodeling of FBC Allison and then I vividly remembered Id.

The night that church burned is the night that I changed forever. After all that I saw: supernatural or not, I can never go back to my former ignorance.

Despite the terrifying events that followed my previous visit, I found myself approaching the far end of the cemetery, and there, a blackened statue loomed.

"For the record," I began, "I am not praying! Despite what your devotee would argue."

The burnt statue of Christ received my procession in silence, so I continued.

"Henry seemed to think it ironic that I'd come and talk to you but still deny your divine presence. Well, it's been some time, but I feel like I could do with a little bit of creative expression, and I'm certain that my eh... hobby is not religious at all but is unabashedly philosophical."

Silence.

"Yes, your mute focus does give me leave to freely articulate. I thank you for that. Uninterrupted verbal processing is good for the... erm soul. Speaking of which, if I affirm the existence of the human soul, do I have to also affirm the existence of a creator of that soul?"

No response.

"I imagine that you would assert that those concepts are united. You see, I wrestle with this thought. Can the human soul exist, simply through the evolution of man? Was every preexisting state of being prior to the homo-sapiens incapable of the attributes that we use to define the soul? If so, what sparked the change in our species? Or must the soul's very existence demand acceptance of a Designer? I suppose that the first question I should ask is, 'What constitutes a soul?'"

I bathed in the silence, steeping over my own questions. After several moments of musing in the dark, I began again.

"Can't I simply accept the unknown and not be held accountable for truths that are beyond my scope? Why must—" A deep voice behind cut off my thought.

"Weeeell, I'd like to think that the soul *is* the existence of the person." My skin immediately hiked up like a frightened cat's fur, but the speaker continued in his bellowing drawl.

"So, if man exists, and realizes that he exists, and wrestles with the extent to which he exists, doesn't that imply the potential gravity of his existence is something more complex than himself?"

Turning, I began to recognize the speaker's voice.

"And if the true purpose of his existence is something greater than himself, then there must be something greater that exists."

This same nocturnal philosopher had just preached to me about Revelation on Sunday.

"And if there is something greater and more complex than the existence of one's soul, then that Greater must not only be a some*thing*, but a some*one*. For how can mankind be ultimate, if he knows not himself fully?"

The chubby grin of Pastor David Kent met me as I finished rounding about. My chills lessened significantly, but the fact that he was there with me in the cemetery was still greatly unsettling. Despite my shaky nerves, I was able to provide a rebuff.

"But who's to say that the "Someone" is him?" I gestured over my shoulder to the statue.

Pastor Kent stepped forward a pace, his footfall unusually soft (particularly for a man of his girth). His smile became visible in the ambivalent light of the narrow moon. I also began to see the dark jeans and black shirt that he wore. It always takes a moment to recognize someone that you've only previously seen in a formal setting. Seeing him in casual clothes caused me to—for a brief instant—think that he was a different person entirely. After stepping into my bubble, he spoke in a much more intimate tone.

"Out of all the historical figures that you've read in your research, which I can safely assume is extensive, due to the tome you've got tucked under your arm, have you ever encountered another person who both defined and defended the souls of men as much as he? Why would he go to such lengths to ensure that each person he met examined their own soul? What would that profit him?"

"Well, it could be that the crowds were drawn by the novelty of self-betterment. If Jesus knew that the people were living under the physical oppression of the Romans and the moral oppression of the Mosaic law, something that spoke of grace would appeal to them. So, the people listened to his speeches, believed that they could live without having to endure the brow-beating of the priests, and they spent their time dwelling on something intangible that awaited them after death, the irreversible threshold. He found himself with a throng of impassioned hopefuls, and the societal power to question the establishment of their day."

"Well (rich with the southern drawl), that's possible, but why would the people turn on him, if he had persuaded them of ideals that are only good for them?"

Pausing, I knew the answer, but then I saw that the parallel to my own life became clear. "Because they realized that it was too good to be true." Transparently, I felt a twinge of sorrow when I finished speaking.

Pastor Kent must have noticed my forlorn physiognomy, because he took another step closer, squeezed my shoulder and said, "I can't make you believe, Marcus, but your existence is perhaps the best piece of evidence, and your regret substantiates your soul."

I sighed, decidedly finished with the discussion, but also wanting to politely remove myself from arm's reach. The big ole' country boy still had a somewhat imposing appearance, despite the kindly way in which he spoke. I raised my hand to my mouth to usher a subtle cough, and when I tilted my head forward, I noticed that on his hip hung a large knife in its sheath!

I took a step back without thinking. My alarm became irrepressible.

"What are you doing out here at this time of night?" I asked with an anxious voice. "And what do you need that large a knife for?" I suppose, now, that I had decided to dive headlong into confrontation.

The burly reverend looked down at his hip and gave a soft laugh. "Oh, this? Ha, I'm a big knife guy. In every sense of the word!" He laughed, but I just stared, eyes wide and watching his every movement. "No, Marcus, I was just over at the church trying to do some wiring on the new stage. I always take a trusty knife with me when I'm doing construction projects."

I had been tricked one too many times. The niceties of before washed away, and all that was left was that sense of impending doom. I backed away till I bumped into the chest of Jesus.

Kent took a step towards me.

"Oh, no, Marcus, I wasn't trying to scare you. I just heard you enter the gate and was curious. I'm sor—"

I didn't stay to listen to the rest of what he had to say. I sprinted around him, irreverently hopping over a few tombstones in my haste, and left through the open cemetery gate. He called after me once, but I kept running back up main street, past the church, past the library, and even past the police station. I had half a mind to run inside and report Pastor Kent, but I knew that unless I had more substantial evidence, they would immediately dismiss him as a real suspect. For the time being, I am truly alone in the investigation.

<u>Henry Paul Loadwain's Journal – 3 July 2023 (1400)</u>

I did something today that I never considered I would have to do. However, after speaking with Grigory the other night I knew that there were uncomfortable questions that needed to be asked. We both reluctantly shared our suspicions back at the fire station, and so I spent this morning exploring possibilities.

Matthew Carlyle, our youngest member of the police department, is notoriously head-strong and impulsive, which is not exactly what I would imagine the now serial killer to characteristically be, but there are interesting points of evidence that have come to light and I can't simply ignore them.

He sat in our interrogation room. His skin was pale, and he bore the look of a whipped puppy. Again, not exactly killer behavior. I would imagine someone who's slain half the town to be stone-cold. He looked like he had indeed been caught in the act of something, but I could not be convinced just yet that it was the murder of thirteen people.

"Thirteen people... if we don't catch this guy soon, Allison will be a ghost town." I said to myself.

With that morbid thought in mind, I pressed the unlock button on the wall panel and pushed the door open. I wore a trained scowl on my face as I entered the room. Matthew went from pale to colorless.

Perfect. I was satisfied with my presentation's effect.

With the clichéd flopping of a manilla folder on the metal table, I began the interrogation.

"Carlyle." That was all that I said as I sat in the chair opposite him. I waited a moment or two, then started to tap my finger onto the file. He had no idea that the file didn't contain anything pertinent to him, but the illusion certainly seemed to make him squirm. After a few uncomfortable moments, he began.

"Henry."

"That's *Captain* to you, Carlyle. When I know that I can trust you, we will be on familiar terms again. But I just don't know what to make of all this evidence."

"What evidence?" Matthew asked in a quivering voice.

I wordlessly tapped on the "evidence" and then deflected with a question that would hopefully keep up the deception.

"Carlyle, why were you at the mayor's house the night of the fire when you had called in sick that morning from work?"

"I... uh... I..."

My head tilted forward with an eyebrow cocked to skepticism.

"I had heard that there was some commotion at the mayor's house, and I wanted to go and help. The situation seemed more important than my immediate physical needs. With all that's been going on, I was afraid to leave you, Tommy, and Gamble alone against the killer."

"Well, I would love to believe that Carlyle. Like really. That sounds very admirable, but why were you there before the call even came out over dispatch? How would you know to be there?"

His initial response was more stammering. Then he finally summoned an excuse. "Well... Hen— I mean, Captain, I actually was the one who called 9-1-1."

I interlaced my fingers and rested my chin on my thumbs, letting the silence speak for me. I suppose he knew that he couldn't hide that nugget from us. Inevitably, we looked back at the CAD system recording of the caller's phone number, and realized that it was his, even though he chose not to verbally identify himself to the dispatcher. After a few more moments of letting the implications lay on him like a thick blanket, I asked specifically.

"So... since you were on the scene to call for 9-1-1, you couldn't possibly have been responding to a call already made there. Let me ask you again... what were you doing there, at the mayor's house on the night of his murder?"

Matthew was visibly quivering. It was almost sad to see. Almost.

"I... uh..."

"Again with the 'I... uhs'? Let me ask another question to help jog your memory? What was Captain Andrews of Allison Fire Department also doing there? He, by the way, also conveniently called out of work that day."

At this point, Carlyle looked as though he was about to faint. It seemed that whatever he was fighting to conceal was bubbling to the surface.

"I want a lawyer."

Crap. I rapped my knuckles on the table to subdue my frustration.

"You'll have one. I just need you to do one more thing for me."

"'Kay" he said reluctantly.

I briefly left the room and came back with a Bible in hand.

Carlyle looked at the book with curiosity. He studied me with anxiety as I set the book on the table. Slowly, I slid it toward him. He didn't seem to recoil as it got closer. I took that as a good sign but had to make sure. I flipped open to a random page, trusting that any portion of Holy Scripture would be sufficient to harm a demon.

"I need you to put your hand on this book and promise me that what you've said is true, then read that sentence there. Obviously, I'm just wanting you to affirm your details following where you lied to me and I have since called you on it. With your hand on this Bible, promise that you spoke the truth about calling 9-1-1, then read."

He looked at me in bewilderment but then slowly lifted his hand. I stared intently at him as he touched the Bible. Nothing happened. He promised in the manner that I asked him to then read from Ecclesiastes.

"Thank you, Matthew. You'll get your lawyer, but you are suspended for abusing sick time and lying to a superior. We'll be in touch."

He was dumbfounded for several seconds. Then he shook himself and said, "Yes sir." Without another word, he got up and walked out.

Gamble's voice came over the speaker. "What the Hell was that all about? What's with the book?"

I chuckled as I stood up and made my way for the door. Gamble buzzed me out using his button in the observation room. He met me in the hallway and leaned against the wall.

"It was just a little test." I said, dismissively. I knew that Gamble didn't believe in the supernatural.

"Yeah? That book supposed to make him a man of integrity, all the sudden? He just lied to you, like, thirty seconds prior. You should fire that little turd."

Gamble had become so direct throughout his budding career at APD. I suppose after we lost Alex and Samwell, he just stopped putting up with the bull-crap. Without God, this job would form me into a bitter man as well. But like me, Gamble was forced to assume responsibilities that he hadn't been fully equipped for. Keeping that in mind, I tried to show him a little extra grace.

Gamble studied me, glanced at my Bible, then looked down the hallway.

"Well... are you ready to roll into the next interview?"

After a deep breath of anticipation, I let it out in a sigh.

"I suppose so."

This next interview was one that I felt much less confident about.

†

Captain Andrews walked into the interrogation room with poise. He, unlike Carlyle, didn't seem the least bit concerned that he was a suspect in the murder of thirteen people. Nor did he seem fazed by my silent stares. That elevated level of confidence could mean a couple different things. He could be innocent, and he knows it, so he fears no judgement. Or... he's guilty, but clever enough to know that we don't actually have any evidence on him. Either way, his smug demeanor was annoying.

"Andrews." I began.

"Loadwain." He returned with an obnoxious grin.

"Why were you at the may—"

"Henry, are we really gonna do this? You and I both know how the system works. I'm not actually a suspect here. You have no evidence against me."

"Well... Larry, we kind of do. You see, you were observed fleeing the scene of the mansion fire. You, who were supposed to be home sick from work showed up at the mayor's mansion, hiding beneath a hood, walking away from the site of an explosion, mere yards from the corpses of two security guards." Still, Andrews was implacable.

"Henry, you have no proof that I was there."

"I had an eyewitness identify you."

"Grigory."

His response was so quick that I was caught off guard. I didn't know what to say.

"The witness is anonymous," I finally said.

"Don't be stupid, Henry. I know it was that aggravating foreigner. He's been a thorn in my side since he joined."

"At one point, I thought that y'all were friends. Y'all have been through some harrowing stuff together."

"If you count nearly dying in multiple situations that are completely his fault, you're right, we have been through some harrowing stuff. The reality is that he is a troublemaker."

"Well, right now, you're the only troublemaker I'm worried about. What were you doing there? And don't give me that crap about seeing the urgent need and showing up. I've already heard that tune tonight."

Andrews chuckled.

"You see, Henry, this whole situation is so... inconsequential. It doesn't really deserve my attention."

"Oh, I'm sorry that you've got something more pressing than possibly being charged with the murder of thirteen people and the arson of two different structures."

"Henry, I didn't kill them. I haven't killed anyone. This is a waste of time."

"Then what were you doing rendezvousing with Officer Carlyle at the mansion."

"Come now, this is ridiculous. I don't have time for this."

I had heard and seen enough to alert my deeper suspicions. Looking down, I realized that I left my folder and more importantly, my Bible on the hallway table.

Standing up, I acted like I was going to concede. "Fine, Larry. I just need you to do one small favor for me. I'll be right back."

He scoffed as he sat there with his arms crossed.

I exited the room and approached the small table that held my Bible and the folder. Just then, I heard a commotion down the hall near the front entry way.

Turning, I saw Mark waving frantically and Tommy trying to hold him back.

"Mark, you can't go back there." Tommy warned.

"Henry, Henry, there you are! Henry, I've found something important. I need to talk to you right now!"

I approached the front desk and patted Tommy on the shoulder.

"Thanks Tommy. What is it, Mark?"

Mark straightened out his ruffled shirt. "Finally! I've been trying to get ahold of you all day."

"I'm sorry, Mark, I've been busy. What have you got?"

Mark eyed the huffing Tommy suspiciously then gestured for me to sit in the lobby with him, so we could talk in confidence.

"How well do you know your pastor?"

The implications of the question immediately slapped a look of skepticism on my face.

"Mark, you can't seriously be thinking that David Kent is the killer?"

"Answer the question, Henry. How well do you know David Kent?"

I thought earnestly, despite the irritation welling up within that Mark would even consider accusing someone I loved and trusted.

"I mean, I've known him for years. He's been my pastor since I graduated high school. He's not only a spiritual leader, but he's also a dear friend." I realized that I could go on and on, saying good things about David, but my frustration came to a head. "Why are you asking this, Mark?"

Mark looked sorrowful as he listened to me speak so well of his suspect. Slowly he asked, "Did you know that your pastor has some skeletons in the closet?"

My eyebrows furrowed. "What kind of skeletons?"

Mark opened his mouth to speak when I heard a familiar sound in the distance. My head snapped up as I instinctively sought the origin of the noise. Metal sliding on metal, like the push of a door bar. Immediately, I shot to my feet and ran for the back door. I nearly smacked into the observation room door as Gamble stepped out.

"Henry?" He asked in surprise.

I jumped around the door and kept running down the hallway.

"Henry!" Gamble called again after me.

I pushed out the back door of the station and looked around the alley to find Captain Andrews. He was gone.

"Henry, chill out!" Gamble said, as he jogged up to me. "He's a free man. He said that there's not sufficient evidence to detain him, so he was free to leave if he wanted to. He left his phone number if we've got any more 'riveting questions', as he called them."

"Why'd you let him go, Gamble!?" strain evident in my voice.

Gamble looked shocked. "Because I had to, Henry. He was right."

I looked back down the long stretch of hallway, realizing now how bizarre I must have seemed. Gamble, Tommy, and Mark all stared at me. No one said a word. I felt that I looked like a fool, and the fact that they all gaped at me with slack jaws made the shame worse. My mind was racing. I took a deep breath to yell, but then let it go. I turned to the rear door in silence and stepped out seeking clarity in the open night air.

The Fifth Hunt

The time of the hunt is fast concluding. I must now do something loftier, something... purer. The season of isolated kills is almost passed. Today, I will pile the slain. These pestilent creatures have spread their disease far enough!

"*Eradicate.*"

The word drummed to a rhythm in my mind with the strained pulsing of engorged blood vessels.

"*Eradicate.*"

The master of the house whispers that the end draws near. No filthy rats can remain. Of course, the elder rat will perish, along with the last of the prey. Too easy.

"*Eradicate.*"

Yes, Master, I will! Let them scurry into their hole. Let them cluster and feed. Little do they know that they feast on death. And I will smile as I spit in the face of our enemy.

"*Eradicate!*"

The voice roared through me like the torrent but followed the Hell-sent storm with a whisper.

"*Then we begin.*"

Marcus Spasmen's Notation of Religious Platitudes
from a Potential Killer – July 9th, 2023

Henry did not heed my warnings about Pastor David Kent being a suspect in the murders. That's just as well. I'm currently attending church again — obviously remaining in the safety of the crowd— feigning religious interest so that I might analyze the suspect. He may presume that he has power over this audience, but in reality, he is trapped in place under my watchful eye! If he is the killer of thirteen people and he's still bold enough to stand before an audience and preach of divinely imposed moralities… there has got to be some serious cognitive incongruencies. Or… he's that perfect of a manipulator. I mean, think of how smooth talking he was when we first met. And why was he so jovial to find me alone there, in the cemetery? What cracks in his façade will I observe today? I plan to write actively through the rest of the morning's service, so that I can describe every detail as it happens. I shan't forsake an iota!

The music today is equally sappy. Almost every song rounds off with a key change, then a final verse about experiencing God face-to-face. You would think that the audience would get tired of singing on and on about a near identical experience. Henry is crying again. Maybe not quite the water works he had last week, but still leaking from his eye for sure.

I do have one aggravation to admit while this older layman prays at the commencement of the message. I… I might have been a little presumptuous before… that remote detonating device that I once boasted in discovering… well, I've spotted another one. This one, however, had wires still running out of the aforementioned black box. The wires led right to the ears of the music minister, then one jutted down beside his cheek to form… a microphone. It pains me to admit a back-step like this, but I suppose that my journey of enlightenment has proceeded somewhat divergent from its expected avenue.

Frankly, I've entirely given up the notion of denying the supernatural. I think I can readily admit that I've seen and experienced too much. I don't need to disprove the inhuman attributes of the case of the Hunter or the case of Id, but it does urge me forward to find answers to the unarticulated facets of the cosmos. So, ultimately, I won't consider the identifying of this microphone too much of a loss.

Ah, finally, the old dog has stopped rambling, and here comes the killer. His belly protrudes from the midst of his sports coat. I do clearly visualize (in my mind's eye) the slender appearance of the shade that I once watched kill Mr. Simm. This preacher could be wearing a fat suit. It would be an effective disguise, but how long could he keep it up? I suppose he would eventually show up one Sunday after a couple weeks' vacation, slim and trim, stating that he started on one of those miracle weight loss pills and had been on the carnivore diet. I digress.

He approaches the flimsy music stand of a podium with such ease. It sickens me to think that a murderer could stand in front of all these poor, confused people and only castigate them further for not being religious enough. "Work, work, work", "do, do, do", "bad, bad, bad", "shame, shame, shame", and so on. Maybe Christianity itself is what brought Kent to the murderous state that he's in. Well… *probably* in. I don't have solid proof yet, but soon, I'll know for certain who murdered all those people.

Kent wrapped his chubby fingers around the aluminum podium again and began to speak.

Today's message is about Revelation chapter 12, verses 7-12. I'm not going to write out the sermon outline like I did before. My attention is not so much drawn to the presentation as it is to the presenter. I will grant that the message is about the beast or the "dragon" fighting a war in heaven with the archangel, Michael. The fairy tale is not proving to be pertinent beyond serving as an example to the eccentricity of Kent. He's nearly shouting as he reads these verses, and he's beginning to weep as he reads about the "salvation, and power, and the kingdom." His exposition has been interesting, but also unsettling, given that I know the truth. How could a man who narrowly avoided being charged with assault and battery stand here and preach about salvation, and "the kingdom"?

I know his hidden crimes because several days ago, I started observing Pastor Kent going in and out of a small side room in the library whenever I would come to read. I tried to remain inconspicuous as I watched him from behind a book, across the main room. He had evidently been using the space for a temporary office, at the courtesy of the Priverly woman. One day, when Mrs. Priverly was outside cleaning the sidewalk, and Pastor Kent stepped out for lunch, I managed to slip inside the usually locked room. It's astounding the incendiary content people will leave available for review in journals that they employ to commune with their imaginary deity. He mentioned in the journal, his regret for the violence he once committed, but he also mentioned the internal struggle with more urgings to act out upon his violent tendencies. He described it, "an ever-present culling to slip into loathsome release." That sounds a little unstable to me. To me, that sounds like he's someone whose thirst for violence was not satiated with that one instance of assault and battery.

Speaking of thirst, he's finally done jabbering about the end times and now he's moved over to the table with the elements of communion. The ornate table that was once used to hold the elements burned with the church. So, for today, they're using this plastic folding table with a white sheet over it. I suddenly feel this sinking in the pit of my stomach, realizing that since I'm not going to partake in their mystical observance of crackers and grape juice, my abstinence will probably be noticed and scowled at.

Oh, I know I shouldn't be bothered by the opinions of others, but something still nags at me. I'm happy, at least, to be tucked in the back corner of the audience. Mom and Dad haven't noticed me yet. Henry and Misty are sitting near the middle row. Ole' Grigory and his girlfriend are seated next to them. I'm essentially a fly on the wall here. Me and whoever this is looking on from the second-floor balcony. They're not partaking either. Just looming... with a hood on... watching intently as Kent and

the congregation raise the juice cups to their mouths... Oh God—

CHAPTER 6

Private Journal of Grigory Yakor – (2314) 9 July 2023

"Do this in remembrance of me." Those words will carry the world's weight to them now. They should have carried it already, I suppose, considering that Jesus was speaking of His imminent sacrifice, but somehow, I never gave much thought to that expression, even though I had heard it countless times. Now, I hear in my memory, Brother David Kent saying it, just before the momentary silence of everyone drinking from their juice cups, then Henry's startling shout toward the crowd. It was in the next moment... that the horror began.

It started out with a cough here or there across the library. Henry's outcry and my abrupt slapping of the cup out of Lia's hand caused some people to look on us in confusion, but by the time our seat neighbors leaned in to ask if we were alright, heavy wet coughs rose throughout the room. People stopped paying attention to our outbursts and became suddenly aware of the unusual nature of the coughing.

Glen Sanders, a banker and father of three teenage girls was the first to vomit a geyser of blood and collapse into a chair. Those who weren't coughing themselves cried out at the sight.

Victoria Evans, the leader of the senior ladies Sunday School class fell and struck her head against the edge of the chair behind her before landing face down in her own red emesis. At this, the room erupted, realizing that some unidentified danger was in their midst.

Far down the center aisle, Kenneth Brussel, a youth boy awaiting the start of his senior year, gagged and fell to the ground crying, blood running freely from his mouth. I ran to the boy and tried to tend to him while pulling my phone out to call dispatch. The boy grabbed me in sheer panic. I tucked the phone between my shoulder and cheek while turning the deteriorating boy to his side, so that he wouldn't aspirate on his vomit. I tried to calm him as he continued to regurgitate. Then, I finally heard dispatch answer.

"Carey, it's Grigory with Allison Fire. We've got some kind of chemical attack at the library, during church hours! I think—"

I stopped speaking. Kenneth was no longer moving. I felt for a pulse. There was none.

I flung him onto his back and was about to begin CPR when another body hit the floor right next to the boy. Howard Brussel, Kenneth's father lay motionless, his eyes were rolled back and he had red, frothy sputum flowing from his mouth.

I was too in shock to think straight. I stood up, shivering all over and raising my hands to my head. My wide eyes filled with tears as I faced the nightmare around me. There were so many people that I knew and loved collapsing in convulsive heaps everywhere. Chairs were knocked over on top of some of the twitching or the deceased. Wives clung to their lifeless husbands. Husbands roared over the still frames of their wives. Women wailed in agony as they clutched their children who would never grow up. Mary Kent wept over the corpse of David, who had fallen back and crushed the makeshift communion table. Wooden bookshelves were plastered with viscous red ooze.

I looked back to where I had been sitting. Lia seemed healthy, but she and Henry were kneeling over someone else. My vision blurred for a moment, realizing that Misty lay there dying, and Henry was watching her suffer!

My ears throbbed with the cacophony of screams and retching and groans and gags. My head pounded to the beat of a thousand drums. I looked about the room once more and finally noticed a hooded man on the second floor of the library, he stood motionless, arms raised, and a smirking chin jutting out from the shadow of the cowl. I never heard what Carey was saying to me. I just finally spit out what I needed to say.

"The Hunter is here, and he has poisoned the church!" I dropped the phone and took a step toward the staircase when I saw the figure turn and run. He was being pursued by none other than Mark Spasmen! Mark roared after the man, completely hysterical! They both plowed out the side emergency exit toward the fire escape. I almost stepped off in pursuit, but something held me back.

"You are needed here." I felt something deep inside me say.

I looked over to Misty who was sitting up at last, her back against Henry's knee but she had a trickle of blood running down the side of her mouth and appeared deathly pale.

I nodded my head, wiped my tears, and did the thing that no firefighter would ever wish to do. Swiping a marker from the pen cup at the library counter, I began triaging my church family for a mass casualty incident.

"If you can hear me, and you're able to walk. I need you to exit the library!" I shouted with a cracking voice. "Please wait in the parking lot!"

A few heads nearby looked up. One or two people assented and staggered toward the exit.

"HEY! IF YOU CAN WALK, GET OUT OF THE ROOM, GO WAIT OUTSIDE! HELP IS ON THE WAY!"

After that screaming command, a couple-dozen people began to stir and they made their way toward the parking lot.

Finally, it's time to go to work!

†

"Black" written on a pale, motionless forehead.

Next victim, female in late forties, no pulse – "Black."

Next, male in early fifties; I palpated only a carotid pulse. Agonal breathing with four breaths per minute – "Black."

Next, seven-year-old pediatric male: had a pulse of forty-nine bpm with shallow, inconsistent respirations, approximately six breaths per minute. – "Black."

Дepмo. How could I?

But he was "expectant." There was nothing I could do. If I gave all my attention to him, I would have forsaken all the others that had yet to be checked. Lock it down. Keep moving.

Next, female in late seventies; work of breathing was labored, but consistent. Her radial pulse was elevated. Her skin was dry but pale. She was disoriented, unable to focus or use coherent words. One pupil was constricted and one was dilated. Unilateral drooping of her lip. Possible stroke. – "Red"

Next, female, early thirties; labored work of breathing, her pulse was thready, her skin diaphoretic, responsive to verbal stimulus. Minimal indication of blood loss or poisoning. – "Red" Thank God, Misty was ok for now, but she would be a priority transfer. Henry of course, ignored my request for all the "Green" tags to step outside and he hovered like a fly over my assessment. Lia didn't listen either.

"Have you trained in Mass Casualty Incident Triage?" An odd question to ask your girlfriend.

She shook her head with wide-eyes.

Ok, I'm going to keep writing colors on their heads. If they're Red, watch them closely, support them in what way you can, we've got an AED, pulse ox, BVM, and stethoscope in that hallway. Don't let the Reds become Black. If they're Yellow, don't let them become Red. When the ambulances get here, Reds will go first.

She nodded. I didn't have time to make sure she got all that. I nodded back and resumed my work.

Next, a male in his early eighties who was knocked down against the wall during the pandemonium. I lifted a bookshelf off his leg. He was alert and oriented. He had a strong pulse, and regular work of breathing. Non ambulatory with an extremely swollen and discolored knee. – "Yellow"

"Mr. George, you are going to be ok!" The old man simply nodded with tears in his eyes. He turned his head, and I followed his gaze. Silent tears fell while we stared at the soulless frame of the seven-year-old boy.

Keep moving!

I squeezed my eyelids tight to push out the tears, patted Mr. George on the shoulder and kept on working.

Female, early sixties, lying face down, over a pool of clumpy red. "Oh God." I realized that it was Mrs. Spasmen: Mark's mom. – "Black". Mr. Spasmen sat slumped next to her, whispering. "No Cindy. Not yet, baby." He rocked as he held her slack shoulders. "No Cindy. Not yet, baby."

"Mr. Spas—"

A persistent hushed cry, "No Cindy. Not yet, baby."

I didn't have the heart to pull him away. I gently squeezed his shoulder and then wrote "Green" on his forearm.

I told myself that I would just have to remember the three Greens I had inside. Rising to my feet, I turned my head to scan for anymore witnesses when the doors were flung open and APD, AFD and JMS stormed into the room. I ran to brief them and direct JMS toward my Reds. One ambulance crew took the seventy-something suspected stroke patient. The other stretcher was being pushed by Gary. I helped load up Misty. Lia and Henry piled in the back of the ambulance. Gary almost protested but then realized that it was no use.

He's usually turning these patients over to Lia when the ambulance arrives at the hospital anyway. And only a fool with a death-wish would try to separate Henry from his bride. I set Misty up with vitals on the monitor while Gary started an IV and began pushing fluids. I looked at Gary and Lia, then out the back window to the chaos of the library. Misty was well cared for. I needed to get back to work.

Squeezing Henry's shoulder, I leaned in and said, "She's going to be ok."

That's a dangerous claim to make in EMS, but I trusted in all the hands tending to Misty. He didn't look up, he just nodded and sat right beside the stretcher on the bench seat, eyes wide and fixed on his bride. I quickly stole a kiss on Lia's cheek then hopped out the side door of the ambulance. Gary gave me a wink and then I closed the door. I could see him shout to the EMT driver through the cab window. "Let's move!"

I began walking quickly toward the library entrance, while being pelted in the back of the head by gravel. I almost reached the door when someone stepped out from the side of the building.

It was Mark. He didn't acknowledge me. He, himself, looked to be in a sort of stupor.

"Uh, Mark?"

He didn't heed me at all.

I ran up beside him as he stepped up to the threshold of the door. His face was swollen and bleeding!

"Mark! What happened?"

It finally clicked in my head, that he had chased down and evidently faced the Hunter!

Still, Mark didn't respond. He took two steps inside the door then fell to his knees. I knelt beside him.

"Mark, what's wrong?"

His eyes were red, and full of tears. Suddenly, he began to wail. I looked forward and then bowed my head in sorrow. Not ten feet from where we knelt was the rigid body of his mother, softly being rocked in the arms of Mr. Bryce Spasmen who still whispered, "No Cindy. Not yet, baby."

Marcus Spasmen's Account of Facing His Demons – (11:24 PM) July 9th 2023

I know now that I was never truly acquainted with loss. Nor had I ever met real hatred face-to-face... until today. I want to grieve and be free of this pain. The morosity has somehow inundated every part of my life. Fond memories are tainted by this anguish and all my future plans suddenly feel vaporous. They are no longer worth the attempt to grasp. Seeing her there, exanimate and empty... it fogs my mind, it rips at my heart. Things just don't make sense like they once did! My motivation to do anything is entirely absent, save for a new ravenous desire to butcher that man.

But nearly parallel to my thirst for revenge is the occurrence of spasmodic twinges of shameful intrusion. "Why couldn't I save her?" "Why didn't I notice the irregularly carbonated communion cups?" "Why couldn't I have reacted quicker like Henry and Grigory did?" "How—how could I let my own mother die?"

I know it can't all be my fault. That damnable religion is truly to blame! If mom hadn't been so committed to those delusions, she wouldn't have taken part in their ordinance, nor would she ever have been on the list of the Hunter's targets. If there is a God, he detested what was being done there. Otherwise, he wouldn't allow his followers to be massacred like that. My mother always touted that "God protects His children," but *He* failed to protect her. If anyone's loyalty justified protection, it was my mother's. She was indeed the best person I've ever known.

I knew that something was wrong as soon as I beheld the hooded man leering down over the crowd. I couldn't afford a complete view of his face at that point, but I knew that he didn't belong amongst the congregation. Something deep down told me that this man was the Hunter, even before anybody in the room started dying. It was as if evil enveloped him. As a flashlight floods a room with luminance, that man's presence emanated shadow. As others raised their communion cups to their mouths, I rose to my feet and felt the irrepressible urge to run to him. Regardless of whether I had any clue of what I was going to do when I reached him, my mind had already been made up.

Leaving my seat, I rounded the stairs on the far side of the room. I reached the landing in-between floors when I began to hear gagging and coughing. I paid little heed to the sounds as I continued my climb. I reached the top of the stairs, then I heard screams from the room below. I looked ahead and saw him there, the hooded man, the Butcher of Allison. The smile that once jutted from beneath the cowl disappeared and he mouthed an expression of shock, before resuming a grin that was all the crueler. The grey hood then gestured to the room below with a sideways nod.

That was when I leaned over the rail and saw my father, stumbling down toward the ground as he tried to hold up Mom. "Cindy, Cindy? You're going to be ok!" I felt a pull to turn and go back down to help them. That's what I should have done, but something inside me snapped in that next moment.

The Hunter looked at her and then returned to me with an exaggerative frown. His frown soon faded and a smile crept back on his face, but something inexplicable happened in that instant. This smile was distinctly different. The lips curled back unnaturally, and the canines appeared more pronounced. Something carnivorous stood there within the human frame of that grey robe.

My breathing was so loud that it drowned out the screams of the dying below. The enemy stood before me and mocked my mother's death. I was, at last, resolved to tear him apart with my bare hands.

"It's time, my little nail." He said with a low growl that rumbled its way into my mind, despite my heavy breathing and the horrific tumult below. At that instant, I lost all sense.

I ran at the butcher, not caring that he certainly had the magmatic dagger on him somewhere; not caring that his victim-tally was in the dozens; not caring that I was most likely about to join that tally. Regardless the cost, I was going to kill the Hunter.

He wore that monstrous grin even as he turned and ran for the fire escape. His arrogance infuriated me! I found myself roaring at the loathsome creature! He slammed the metal push-bar open and turned to climb down the fire escape. In a few seconds, I caught that door and slung it wide again. When I turned to descend the metal steps, he was already across the street. I bounded down the stairs and sprinted across the unusually quiet road, a distinct antithesis to the nightmare taking place inside the library.

He continued past the *Daily Bale* and ripped headlong into the woods behind Main Street where the first sign of the coming factory had just been placed. I followed him, my breathing so heavy, so full of both vivacity and aggression, I didn't let up. We sprinted in this manner, like two animals caught in a woodland chase. He never even glanced back at me, he just pressed on, like a locomotive. Any branches that jutted out amidst his path were snapped by his very passing. His gossamer movements transported him before me to a dense wall of brush that gave no impeding to his retreat. He disappeared on the other side of the foliage and I braced for impact as I feverishly sped up and charged through the verdant wall.

†

Fighting the resistance of thickly suppled branches and shrubbery, I leaned forward into the clearing. My weight carried me through the opening as I crashed to the ground unceremoniously. I rose to my feet, the hunger for conflict surging like victorious waters over a crumbled dam. I whipped my head all about me, expecting the Hunter to be prowling at my back, prepared to strike. At that moment, I paid little heed to the bewildering fact that it was nighttime already when I reached the meadow. Mere moments before, I had been running through the woods that flitted with daylight. I continued to scan the twilit realm. Suddenly, my eyes shot forward, and in the midst of the open meadow, there stood the Hunter.

His back was turned to me, and his gaze evidently transfixed on the crater that had long been the source of such curiosity. I approached, shoulders heaving and fists clenched white. It was time to end this.

When I had reached mere yards from him, I saw his hand suddenly alight in flame. The dagger that had unleashed Hell on so many was now glowing in preparation to bear me hence.

Let him try, I thought.

Hell itself wouldn't stop me from killing this man.

"Are you ready, Marcus?" the growling voice asked from within the cowl.

I cracked my knuckles and rolled my head around to loosen my neck.

"Are you?" I growled back.

The crater before us suddenly ignited, as tongues of orange flame burst from its epicenter. Charred shrivels of flower petals flew into the air amidst indiscriminate embers. As the morning-glories burned, a faint squeal pierced the glen, as if a colony of tiny living beings suddenly met a horrid fate. My once-hardened jaw now slacked, and I took a cautious step back from the blaze.

"Oh, I've waited an eternity for this, Marcus."

This time, the Hunter's voice didn't growl like some sepulchral deity, but instead spoke in a familiar tone. I gasped as the butcher turned toward me and pushed back his grey hood with his free hand. His thick auburn hair absorbed the colors from the flames and all the malevolence of the inhuman grin that I saw in the library was married —in an instant— to the familiarity of a friend's face. He had shaved his beard, which gives reason as to why I didn't recognize Gamble immediately.

"It's time, my little nail."

"Gamb— Bu— What?" I couldn't collect my thoughts enough to form a coherent question.

"How could yo— Wha— Why?" I was shaking uncontrollably.

"It all started here, you know." He began, flicking the fiery blade around like a conductor's baton as he stepped along the rim of the crater. "This is where we met."

In my head, I suddenly thought through those words and realized their inaccuracy. Gamble and I had met in town, when he had presumed that I was Id and arrested me for the abduction of Merrin Clemmens.

Edward Gamble continued, "This is where I found what I had been looking for... who I had been looking for. I found my salvation."

"Oh great, another religious zealot." I said aloud in spite.

"This blade brought him to me, like a beacon. He found me, changed me, and gave all that I desired."

Despite my disdain for the religious jargon, its familiar effect on Gamble made my skin crawl.

"Id?" I asked with a faltering voice.

"No, no, no... Rasha-Chatta was a child. Impatient, petulant, and self-interested." His voice was interlaced with the deeper tone of another: I presume the spirit's. Their speech seemed flowed in other-worldly unison.

"What the Hell did you just say?"

"Listen, Marcus. You and I are a part of something much bigger than the vain ambition of one archdemon." Gamble's words were manic.

"Archdemon?" I asked with palpable skepticism. "I thought you were the guy who trusted only in what you saw with your own eyes."

"And now my eyes have seen so much, Marcus. So much..."

"Right... but if I'm part of your big plan —that I'm about to kill you for, by the way— why were you trying to persuade me of a strictly tangible universe? Why go through all the trouble of keeping me from religion, despite espousing it at last?"

"Ardent skeptics make the most passionate devotees. And you know the best part? They don't ever have to know it."

"So why show me your hand at last?"

"Because the end has begun. Hell is at the gate." He turned his head and gestured to the crater that lapped with flame.

He turned back to me, and I recoiled to see the fanged mouth and glowing orange eyes where Gamble's once shone.

"It's too late for you, Marcus. Time to drive the nail into the coffin!"

I fell back, crying as my chest erupted in tremendous pain, and the sensation of imminent death washed over me. Smoke started to rise from within my shirt and a faint orange glow emanated from my chest. Through watery eyes, I watched Gamble stalk toward me, his magmatic dagger pulsing in ever-heightening intensity.

I wailed in agony and tore away at my shirt to reveal the scar that Id had given me all those months ago glowing, like a fire of its own.

"Don't worry, Marcus, I won't kill you… yet. I don't skip steps, like Rasha-Chatta in his greedy haste, but now I can imprison you here. With the vandals dead and the church scattering, we will begin the final rites." With a sharp, almost sensual inhale, he added, "Hell is at the gate."

He raised his free hand and began to somehow pull fire from the crater in a coiling stream. It coalesced in his palm for a moment, then he thrust it forward and the symbol in my chest ignited to meet the blazing current from his hand. Flames burst forth and I could no longer breathe. I tried to move my arms. I tried to roll away, but it felt as though the symbol on my chest was an incredible weight passing through my supine body and driving deep into the soil beneath me. I cried silently, as one does in a nightmare; giving forth every effort to voice my terror, but not a sound was made. I burned alive in mute anguish! I was nailed to the ground by some unseen stake. This was Hell. I was pinned to the gate of Hell. I had at last become the "nail in the coffin."

After what felt like an eternity, the fire went out in my chest and the Hunter spun round to look at the crater that was no longer lit with flame.

"What!?" He roared. The trees about us shaking at the outburst.

I tried again to breathe and felt my lungs fill with cool air.

"Oh thank God!" I cried aloud.

The fanged Gamble gnashed his teeth at my cry. With wide, orange and black globes, he studied between the blackened crater and my burned chest.

"One of the vandals still lives!" He reasoned to himself.

"Vandals?" I asked, half-delirious.

He didn't answer. Instead, the butcher held out his arm and a black cloud of particulates formed in front of him. He entered the pall and vanished from sight. A few moments later, the remaining particulates blew away in the wind.

Immediately, I attempted to roll over and escape but that indominable weight still pinned me to the spot.

"Damnit!" I shouted in desperation. I screamed, calling for help at the top of my lungs for what felt like hours. No one ever came.

With the absence of the fires, night had overcome the glen. The last quarter moon phase seemed somehow suffocated of its natural luminance. Spires of shadow wreathed the meadow. Those pine trees towering overhead made me feel so small and insignificant. Indeed, I am small and insignificant.

"What can I do? I'm nothing compared to these evils! Will I really just lay here as Gamble cleans up whatever loose ends he needs to, then comes back and finishes the job?" I catastrophized to myself, my voice hitting the wall of night above me.

The thickness of the night seemed to lessen slightly, and I began to hear the distant chirping of crickets and the tymbals of cicadas. I suppose that if Gamble takes long enough to get back, I'll just become the buffet dinner for some woodland insect. I'm not sure if I'd pick death by the gout of flame from my chest or being ripped apart piece by piece by a colony of hungry ants. Both sounded terrible, but somehow, I knew that the anguish of that hellfire coursing through me was truly the more horrid of fates.

"What can I do?" I asked again, prompting the crickets and cicadas as my audience. Their insightful response was more chirping and rapid clicking.

I tried to budge again. Nothing.

"I can do... nothing," answering my own question.

Suddenly a voice whooshed through my mind like a high wind.

"Now you're starting to get it, Mark."

I jolted in surprise, drawing my arms to protect my face. I was met with the tingling sensation of a great burden being lifted from my body. It took me a moment or two to process the implication of that, but when I did, I moved my head around to look for who had responded. After carefully scanning, I found no one around. With wide eyes, I rolled over and shot to my feet! After a moment of gathering my bearings, I sprinted off through the woods, making my way back toward town!

Eventually, my navigations were affirmed by the sounds of wails and shouts of commands. Red and blue lights began to flash off the pines around me. I was embraced by daylight as I passed the construction sign and exited the woods. The sight of the library and the rush of first responders in and out of the facility jogged my memory of the first of two nightmares.

I slowed as I approached the side of the library and staggered when reaching the door. My mind became foggy again. Someone called my name from behind, but what I beheld when stepping inside absorbed all my senses. I thought that I had left Hell behind in the woods, but returning to town, it had proved to be waiting for me all along.

<u>Henry Paul Loadwain's Journal – (2317) 10 July 2023</u>

I don't have the time to address my feelings about all that has happened. If I could summarize in a few words the hurricane that I feel inside, I would use words like *disbelief, pain, broken trust, loathing, shame*, and maybe even *fear*. But that's all I'm ready to say about the attack. What I record now, I record out of necessity, while we await discharge from the hospital.

As David was reading the scripture references before everyone partook of the tainted ordinance, I had noticed some excessive carbonation in my sealed communion cup. I thought it strange, but not significant until I looked askance at Grigory and saw him studying his own cup. Out of curiosity, he opened the lid of his juice and swirled the contents quietly.

"Do this in remembrance of me." David finished aloud and raised the cup to his mouth.

I watched as Grigory tapped his tongue with his finger, then let the drop of saliva fall into the cup. Immediately, the juice erupted and changed color, foaming over the rim. Without even looking, he swept his arm to his left, hitting Lia in the face and knocking the untasted juice from her hand.

Alerted to the danger, I spun and swung to do the same, but Misty had already started to tip the cup back. She couldn't have had more than a third of the contents before I sent the cup crashing into the nearest bookshelf. A moment later, the widespread pandemonium began.

†

It felt like an eternity before EMS arrived, but Grigory was quick to do what he could to help. After Misty had been triaged, I rode on the ambulance from the scene with her and Lia. Grigory stayed back to help the others. I know that I probably should have stayed too, but something came over me. I've watched too many loved ones die. I could not abandon my wife in her hour of greatest need. In fact, I couldn't control myself even if I wanted to go back and help the victims, some instinctual force kept me glued to her side. I stayed with her through hospital triage, despite glances of annoyance from some of the nurses. I sat with her in the ER as they pumped her stomach and gave her a steady supply of IV fluids. Following that, Misty was moved to the ICU. She's been sleeping peacefully since the procedure and her blood pressure is steadily improving.

Grigory called after we were transitioned to the intensive care unit and shared with me the earth-shattering news that one of my most trusted officers, Edward Gamble is the possessed Hunter! Grig heard it from Mark, who had been catatonic for several hours following the death of his mother. Mark finally found the sense to speak, and he told Grig about his experience in the woods. The horrors that Mark endured is a topic that we haven't even had time to unpack. I really need to sit down with him, offer both condolences and a listening ear. That would probably do him some good to share his emotional burden, but it also might give us some insight into the demon's purpose.

As soon as I got off the phone with Grig, I hunted down Lia, who was in the ER. I asked her to periodically check on Misty while I went back to Allison to meet up with Grigory. After leaving Huntsville, I called Carlyle (rescinding his suspension out of necessity) and Tommy, telling them to meet me at the department.

As previously mentioned, Misty is resting now, before being discharged, and I've already returned from Allison. First, however, I need to write down what happened when I got back into town.

†

Before seeking any clues that might help us locate Gamble or uncover the Hunter's purpose, I returned to the library and dealt with the accosting from federal agents who wanted to know why my town was "falling apart." After accepting their insults of incompetence and then relinquishing command to them — frankly, I could care less about their opinions— I met with Grigory, Tommy, and Carlyle (who was still under scrutiny). We went together and raided Gamble's house.

The power to the home had long been shut off, so we entered in darkness. We moved in pairs throughout the house with flashlights. I kept Carlyle with me, so I could watch him. We moved throughout the house, stepping over rat droppings and dead insects littered across the floor. The home reeked of spoiled meat and the smell grew stronger the further we went into the house. Carlyle and I proceeded down the undecorated hallway and turned right at the first room we encountered.

Opening the door to a small bathroom, we were struck with the pungent smell of untended death. Carlyle gagged, and my eyes watered as I tried to repress a cough. Shining the light in the bathroom, I revealed red streaks across the floor. The volume of blood in the streaks increased the closer they got to the tub, which was behind the door. I stepped inside, my pistol drawn and aimed.

What I found was the bloated corpse of a deer, flies buzzed inside and around a throat that had been torn open and scorched. I was certain that I knew what implement he used to do that.

"Ugh, gaw!" Carlyle gagged again. I passed by him, snatching him on the shoulder and dragging him out of the bathroom. We entered the next room on the right and found a small study. There were a couple dozen books on the shelves, some legal, some historical, some religious.

I had never known Gamble to be a religious man. Any time I broached the topic with him he avoided it like the plague. There's no way he can doubt now. It's a tragic irony that the man who actively disbelieved in the devil is now serving him. That seems the way of things. Those who avoid the supernatural end up running headlong into it, eventually.

At the desk beneath the bookshelf, I saw a stack of papers. They were each handwritten accounts. These papers were titled "Hunts", "First" through "Fifth." I began to thumb through the Hunts and skim some lines. The writing was ominous, and I felt some strange sense of familiarity the longer I looked at the pages.

"Hey Henry!" Grig called from the other end of the hallway. Carlyle and I left that eerie study in a hurry and joined Tommy and Grig in the kitchen. We all stood around a beat-up looking refrigerator, with spots of rust that had sprouted through the paint. The door was cracked open, and the stench was profound. Tommy shined his flashlight into the humid refrigerator.

Carlyle turned and vomited on the floor. At least he couldn't make the place any more grotesque by adding a little throw-up.

Inside the refrigerator, overbearing every shelf and drawer was the folded-up corpse of some woodland animal. Foxes, squirrels, birds, even another deer (but this one was only a little fawn, whose white spots were flecked with blood).

"What the Hell?" Tommy asked through clenched teeth.

All the sudden, we were aroused from our disgusted stupor by the sound of several car doors slamming shut.

"Aw, crap, it's the feds." I whispered to them. I quickly tucked the letters inside my waistband and draped my shirt over them just as the front door burst open. My team stood there, lights aimed in all different directions, but I kept mine on the fridge, seemingly unconcerned to be caught investigating.

"Good God!" Agent Mixon exclaimed as he stepped into the house that his men had just cleared.

"Sir, APD is here." One of the blacked-out agents in tactical gear said to the three-piece-suited Mixon.

"Oh good, the hillbillies have trampled all over the evidence." His condescending tone complimented the scowl he wore as he sauntered down the hall toward us. "Loadwain, I thought I told you that this was no longer your case."

"You just expect us to stand aside and let the killer wipe out the other half of the town?"

"Why disrupt precedent?" He retorted with a smug grin.

"If we're such hindrances in your investigation, what would you have us do?"

"Maybe get a job at the local drug store, or the library, or maybe even the church. I hear there are quite a few open positions in town." He finished with a snort.

Grigory moved from my side in a flash, but I caught his arm just in time. Gear shifted all around us as five rifles were suddenly aimed at Grig.

"This is not the time for that, brother." I spoke quickly in a hushed tone.

Mixon tilted his head as he looked at Grig.

"Are you even a cop? What are you?"

"I'm a firefighter," Grigory said with a cold stare.

"Oh, that's cute, kid. Why don't you go sit in the corner and play with your hose till something catches fire."

Grigory's nostrils flared and the silent tension was so taut that a mosquito's bite would have snapped the suspense and ended in a blood bath.

After a few moments of silence, I patted Grig's arm and looked at Agent Mixon.

"You're right. I don't feel like getting in a pissing contest with you big city agents. Just please try not to get yourselves in a pickle." I gestured for my guys to head to the door. One by one, our assembly of APD and AFD filed out the front door. No agents awaited us outside. I reached for the doorknob to close it on the way out, but before I did I added, "Because if you get your shiny SUVs stuck in the mud, us ole' backwoods hillbillies will have to pull your sorry butts out." I gave a wink and closed the door.

"Begin searching. I'll be right back." Mixon called from inside. His footsteps grew louder until I heard his hand grip the doorknob and the door opened. He stepped forward and closed the door behind him.

"Loadwain, what were you doing here?" He leaned in close, "What did you find?"

"I thought you fellas already knew everything. Why ask me?"

"Don't play with me, you dumb hick! What did you find?"

I smiled at Mixon and asked, "Are all the pieces not fitting into place?" I leaned in closer, "Is there something that all the forensics in the world can't make sense of?"

"Henry, what did you find?" He snarled.

I looked left, then I looked right.

"This is the time for that, brother." I said over my shoulder.

"Wha—" Mixon couldn't even finish his question before Grig materialized from the shadows behind the agent and landed a drum-like punch to Mixon's ribs. The agent crumpled to the ground and began heaving. Grig knelt over the wheezing man, grabbed his shoulder and whispered close.

"Don't worry, you merely have some intercostal bruising. If I had hit you any harder, you might have got a broken rib or wound up with a closed pneumothorax. Treatment for that wouldn't happen out here in the sticks. No-no, you'd have to go to the hospital forty-five minutes away and then wait for a room in the ER. That wait alone could kill you."

"Heeee—" Mixon tried to pull in enough air to capture his breath again, but he was failing miserably. Grigory continued, his voice an octave deeper this time.

"See, if left untreated for long enough, that closed pneumothorax would lead to a complete collapse of the injured lung, then begin to put pressure on your remaining good lung. Tension pneumothorax would take place as any attempt at breathing normally would fail. Your blood pressure would rise and oxygen demand would increase, whilst your actual oxygen perfusion decreased. Your heart would be under too much strain, and the newly filled balloon of a chest cavity would diminish your heart's ability to pump blood. Eventually, your heart would fail to beat entirely, and then... you'd be lying here, dead in the dirt. And your gunslingers inside would stand around with their thumbs up their butts, not knowing how to save you."

Agent Mixon lifted his head, and terrified eyes glinted in the moonlight.

With a chuckle and lighter tone, Grig added, "but what would I know? I'm just a dumb fireman who likes to play with his hose."

At that, we all bolted to the car, howling with laughter as we peeled off, summoning a cloud of dust in our escape down the dirt road.

> *I will add that I had Grig repeat his comments to Mixon for me. I didn't want to leave that out of the record, but I had no idea what he said the first time*

†

It's now 0800, and Misty is awake. She's been here two days, so she gets discharged this afternoon, if the doctor gives the "OK" to her latest bloodwork and last set of vitals. Grig should be here any minute. In his absence, I've used the time to briefly get Misty up to speed on the investigation, catch a nap in the chair, record the above-mentioned experience at Gamble's property, and review the Hunts.

In reviewing Gamble's Hunts, I've found a direct parallel between the animals he describes killing and the human victims that he's murdered. The first few hunts were descriptions of plausible wild game hunts, but the real meaning beneath became clearer as the Hunter's goal was closer to completion. I've noticed that his "craft" becomes more zealous, more ritualistic at each succession, and what was formerly mentioned as some undefined "duty" becomes direct commands from the "Master of the House". This seems like a high-handed slap against God, because in the Bible, in the Gospel of Mark, Jesus used the term "Master of the House" to allude to God's return at the end times. Could all this spiritual warfare in Allison be an indication of the real Master of the House's imminent return?

"Eradicate." He was instructed to eradicate the congregation of FBC Allison. It's terrifying to think that an enemy with these capabilities has been in existence for so long and has yet to do something like poison the communion cups during a church service. These demons could easily do this and much worse at any time, but they are in subjection to their leader's command. And I still believe that their leader cannot act against God's will. But how could the slaughter of His children be in God's will? What greater good gives justification to their murders?

My wisdom fails here. I cannot answer. I don't need all the answers, but I want justice for the evils done, and I want to know that God is indeed in control of all this.

"Eradicate." Is this the final act accomplished by the Hunter? What could be worse than murdering most of my faith community? If I think of Id's attempt at taking dominion, I'm left believing that despite my wishes, this new enemy still has greater evils to perform, but how can we stop it? How can we direct our prayers? And will prayer be the limit of my usefulness?

Oh God, what would you have me do?

Dear God,

I'm prayin' for my family tonight. I guess that I should have been praying for them all along, even before things got really bad. And things have gotten bad. I pray for Momma, that she would be strong as she deals with Daddy. She's been talkin' to You a whole lot lately, which is good, because Daddy's been real hard on her. It makes me mad and sad and confused to see him being so mean. But even still, I pray for Daddy. He hasn't hit Momma yet, but he shoves her now anytime she starts to argue with him. He acts like her talking is hurting his head, so he's trying to push away the noise. He apologizes every time, but Momma isn't going near him now. I've been spanked a lot more now, and for little things. Daddy says that the world outside is dangerous and that we can't trust the people we once did. I don't know what he means by that. Our church family is full of good people. I think we need them really bad right now. I feel like something is here with us in the house. Not like before, but something is talking to Daddy, making him feel so scared. Why doesn't he just talk to You about it, God? Why doesn't he just trust You like he always did? I know my Daddy has been really mean lately, but I know he's still a good Daddy, and I know he still loves You. Please, God, whatever is hurting my Daddy, whatever is making him so scared, please get rid of it.

Lord, I'm just a girl and I don't know a whole lot, but I know that You are stronger than whatever this mean thing is. So please don't let it win.

I hear Daddy slamming the front door. He's mad again.

It sounds like someone just fell on the floor! Oh, he sounds really mad! Make me stron—"

The Sixth Hunt

How close I was to the Master's favor! If only I hadn't let one more target slip. The flame burned bright, the hinges on the gate creaked and the procession of Sheol surged in anticipation… but I failed to kill the leader.

If those who fight to preserve human life lose their inspiration, their resistance will falter, and the flames will rise. Let inspiration give way to despair, and devotion to compromise! The people of Allison will flee, and his church will fail. Death will indeed give way to victory. Not his victory, but ours!

What will they do when the hand that cast the last ballot lies still? My Lord will have justice on the impudent vandals, the enemy's church will have anarchy, and I will have blood… sweet, warm, satisfying blood. I will gorge on their life-force, indulging in the ecstasies of my sanguine victory as all of Hell tramples the landscape.

The rites will be performed, the beast will awaken, humanity will be his fill, and the Master will have dominion at last whilst I imbibe myself on the gore of human sacrifice!

I am the Blood-Warden of Hell, and I bring justice to those who deny my Master's bidding!

<u>Private Journal of Grigory Yakor – (1937) 11 July 2023</u>

Currently, Lia, Henry, and I are all camped out in the living room of Henry's house, tending to the recovering Misty. She returned home this afternoon from Huntsville. She seems to be physically doing well, but there is a dour expression she wears when no one seems to be looking. I imagine that her emotions are all over the place, being the only survivor of those who actually drank the poison. The slower partakers halted before drinking because of the antics that Henry and I displayed. Thank God for that.

Henry's house feels like one of the few safe places left in Allison. Chief Davidson emphatically advised all firefighters to return directly to their homes when leaving shift and keep regular communication with one another until the murderer is caught.

Captain Andrews and Chief Davidson are sequestered at the chief's house in Bear Paw Creek, providing a sort of radio traffic headquarters to monitor and coordinate any activity in town. For my part, I considered offering Cody and Willard a place to stay at my house, but I deemed it best not to risk them becoming victims. Nothing from these Hunts seems to indicate that I'm one of his targets, but he did take one swipe at me already, who's to say that he won't try again. Not to mention, I seem to have this uncanny ability to piss off demons. Therefore, I'd feel much better if my firefighter brothers didn't get involved. But Lia, Henry, Misty, and I are already neck deep in this twisted adventure.

Oh, and Mark! Mark may be farther down the rabbit hole than any of us. He's been through it, that poor man. My convincing had to reach the point of threatening the incineration of his personal library before he finally agreed to come join us here in our "stronghold". I got off the phone an hour ago, at which time he said he was going to make a quick stop before heading this way. He didn't say what he was doing, but I think he went by the public library again. Poor man.

What he described in the woods... it's terrifying.

"The Gates of Hell"? Is the Hunter really trying to bring Hell on earth? How does he plan to accomplish that? What does he plan to do to Mark? Who was there with Mark in the woods after the Hunter disappeared? And who is this "vandal" that he spoke of?

Бог, я знаю так мало!

Henry seems to think that—

†

I just received a phone call from Mark. He's found a letter left by the Hunter! It's labeled "The Sixth Hunt". He said that he's going to send me a picture of it. He said he still had a stop to make. From the background of the picture he sent, I can tell that he's downtown in the cemetery, near the library. Without any further prying, I told him that I understood.

"Just be careful" were the last words I said before hanging up.

Ah, here's the picture.

†

Well, Henry's assertion that each letter successively becomes more ritualistic is certainly founded. The content of this letter seems to be written in a manic delirium. The first letter detailed explicitly step-by-step how he killed the stag (Chief Isaac Knox). This "Sixth Hunt" is almost impossible to follow, as his fixation moves from consuming blood to some beast eating people and even this mention of a "leader" needing to be slain.

And this... "Those who fight to preserve human life." Who is that speaking of? Could it be talking about us? Our entourage; our band of survivors? I presume that Henry would count as our leader but look at this other part.

"Let inspiration give way to despair, and devotion to compromise."

If an inspiring leader falls, people will despair, certainly. But, what devotion fails in the absence of a leader? How does that lead to compromise? What would they be compromising?

Ах! Почему етот демон не может говорить прямо!?

Let me back up. "Their fight will fail..." "*Flames* overcome them..." "Their leader." I should have seen it sooner. Who is the only surviving member of the city council? And who inspires those who fight to preserve life?

Боже мой! I know who the last target is!

Misty Loadwain's Diary – (11:34 PM) July 11th, 2023

Chief Billy Davidson is the final target! The thought raced laps through my mind. I dreaded the fate of my colleague, but I knew that Henry and Grig were better prepared than anyone else to keep him safe.

We had just been discussing the way Gamble's grip on reality seemed to degrade as the Hunts went on. This last account from Gamble seems so ambiguous yet simultaneously foreboding. Grig said that Captain Andrews and Chief Davidson were staged at Chief's house, and they anticipate that the Hunter is headed that way soon. Their plan was to head him off and at last trap the trapper.

I tried not to think of the risk that Henry and Grig were putting themselves in. I was resolved to not simply sit around and worry about them. That would do them no good, nor would it be beneficial for Lia or me. I, for one, couldn't be of any physical assistance. I was still struggling to keep my feet under me. For the time being, I had to simply accept Lia's kind nurturing and just recline on the couch.

Henry and Grigory had just left the house when Lia offered to make us a pot of coffee. Under normal circumstances, I would have gladly taken her up on that because I live off coffee. However, I fear that since the attack at the library, my appetite has been diminished, and strong substances, like caffeine would only aggravate my sensitive digestion.

"Maybe some green tea?" I suggested.

Lia smiled and nodded before energetically responding, "That sounds great! Do you want any honey in it?"

I couldn't repress a smile of genuine appreciation. She was so ready to go the extra mile for anybody. In the back of my mind, the concern that I would become fatigued by her zealous stewardship zipped about my consciousness. However, I soon arrested the thought, knowing the impossibility of being irritated by the sweet girl. Her emotional intelligence is too advanced, and her interpersonal skills too practiced for her to allow herself to become an annoyance. Not to mention that I simply adore the girl! I see plainly why Grig is utterly infatuated with her.

"Honey would be perfect, thank you."

She happily rose and proceeded to the kitchen. I spoke aloud, so that she might hear me across the hall.

"So, Lia, how are things going with Grig?"

I heard the water kettle set in place on the stovetop coil. A moment later, she poked her head back into the room. She giggled softly and failed to fight off a grin.

"I think he's going to propose soon!" She whispered in excitement. As if there was someone else around who might hear the news.

"Wow!" I was genuinely surprised at the timeliness of it, but they are both adults with adult jobs, and I suppose that when you know, you know.

"That's so exciting, Lia. Y'all are perfect for each other. Has he made any comments about rings? Have y'all been talking about getting married?"

She giggled again, "Like all the time!"

I felt longingly for those days of rapturous innocence. It seemed like an eternity since Henry and I were looking at rings, picking out color schemes for our home, and... daydreaming about all the children we would have. May the Lord bless them generously.

I will be satisfied with what He has given. I have Christ, I have enough. Henry is a pretty incredible bonus, too!

"Will y'all move to Huntsville? I imagine that you have no interest in moving to Allison. Especially after all that has happened."

Lia's face darkened. I suppose that mine did as well. How could our thoughts not return to the horrors that our tiny town has suffered? It truly is a testament to her character that she hasn't abandoned Grig and Allison altogether. No, despite everything, she's held fast and performed in the midst of all the trauma. I remember Henry mentioning her hesitation to help when Jonathan was stabbed. I wonder if that was the defining moment for her to no longer hesitate in the face of need. Perhaps her failure that night changed her for the better.

After several seconds, Lia opened her mouth to speak. Her words were interrupted by the rising squeal of the tea kettle on the stove. She never finished her response but instead retreated to the kitchen to pour our tea.

I sat for a moment, stewing on all the evidence that had now come to a head. Then a thought occurred to me.

"Did Grig mention where Mark found the Sixth Hunt?" I asked across the hall.

Lia entered the room with two steamy mugs and a small blue bowl with my wooden honey wand. Her face betrayed piqued interest.

"Yes!" She sustained the "eh" sound for emphasis. "Mark said that he found it in the church cemetery. Apparently, the Hunter had gone to that old statue of Christ in the back of the cemetery and removed the head of the statue. In its place, he set the Hunt and then returned the head of Christ, but this time, left the head turned upside down!"

"Augh, that's awful!" I winced at the blasphemous image.

"I know, isn't that creepy?" Lia said.

"It definitely is." I affirmed. "But you know what bothers me?"

"What?"

"Why would he leave the letter there? The others were hidden in the house, but this one was set out on display. It seems like the Hunter wanted this one to be found. And isn't Mark known for going out to the cemetery and... verbally attacking God?"

Lia's jaw slackened as she listened to my anxious questions.

After a tense moment of silence, she thought aloud, a sense of foreboding in her tone.

"But, why would he leave this note to be found?"

All the lamps in the living room suddenly dimmed, as if they were trying to force their light through a black sheet. My heart began to beat audibly and the hair on my neck stood up as I saw a tall shadow pass from the closet door immediately behind the couch we were sitting on! The darkness seemed to emanate from that being, and all around him succumbed to obscurity as he silently glided across around the couch and rose over us.

"Because I have longed for the chance to be alone with you." A cavernous voice answered.

Both Lia and I were petrified to our seats, unable to speak, unable to flee.

"You see, Misty," the reasoning voice lightened to a familiar tone. "Your death is the beginning of the end. Once I've finally killed the last of the vandals, we will open the gate of Hell. Then, when earth receives its true damnation, I will receive my reward!" The demon's shadowy substance gave way to the normal figure of Edward Gamble. He stood there, eyes pulsing between orange and black, and his canine teeth bared at the emphasis of every word he spoke.

Lia suddenly roused from her shock and thrust her foot against the outside of Gamble's knee. A gut-wrenching popping sound echoed across the room as the Hunter crumpled sideways to the floor. Lia jumped away over the arm of the couch, because as Gamble fell, he drew that horrid dagger. It ripped through the air as he swung it toward Lia.

She managed to jump out of the way in time. I tried to stand and fight, but I fell back and nearly fainted. I saw stars float across my vision, but behind those stars, Gamble crawled toward me, eyes flaring in intensity and the glowing blade was raised!

I pushed myself off the side of the couch and began to back away to the far corner of the room. I screamed aloud. The Hunter began to swing his weapon toward me just when Lia dove over top of him and grabbed the arm that held the knife. She tried to pin that arm down and beat the weapon out of it. Punch after punch after punch, she struck his hand. Gamble's face betrayed a swirl of agony and rage.

Suddenly, with his free left hand, he swung it back and smacked Lia so hard she went sailing into the window and shattered the glass. She fell to the ground, unconscious.

I yelled in terror and pushed myself to my feet. I wobbled for a moment, but Gamble was evidently busy tending to his injured leg. I took a step toward Lia when I heard another pop, much like the one that sent the Hunter crashing to the ground. However, this time, as he stood up, his leg was no longer bent out of alignment; it was evidently healed! He grinned at me and twirled the dagger.

"Gamble, this isn't you. You are a good man. I know you." I pleaded as he stalked toward me with death in his leer.

"This is everything I ever wanted. I am more powerful than any other man. I no longer follow the rules that once bound me. I am free!" He raised his hands in a sort of ecstasy.

"No, it's not you! You are a good man, and you wouldn't want to hurt anybody!"

"That is all I've ever wanted." He said in a particularly somber voice.

"Henry loves you! You are like a brother to him." I cried just before he grabbed my throat.

"Human affections are cheap." He began to squeeze. I felt my head get tight and my throat spasm. "These sentiments are irrelevant. Henry will soon see what profit his 'love' affords."

My vision began to narrow to a cone when all of the sudden I was dropped to the ground. Unbeknownst to us, Lia had woken back up and then drove her foot square into Gamble's crotch. I crawled around the staggered killer and began to make my way for my purse in the kitchen. Lia stood up and tipped the tv off the tv stand that was right above where Gamble lay coughing.

It crashed on top of him with a loud crack. She began to try to push the entire wooden entertainment center on top of him when he vanished from beneath the television!

We both stood still for a moment, unsure of what we actually just saw.

With a newfound burst of adrenaline, I turned and ran for the kitchen to get my pistol out of my purse, but when I passed the central hallway that ran straight through the house, he was there!

Again, he wrenched around my throat, but before I lost all ability to speak, I groaned, "Lia *gag* my purse!" He slammed me to the ground and raised his open hand above his head. The fiery dagger appeared there. Lia's footsteps quickly pattered around us. I watched her enter the kitchen and open the purse.

Again, my vision began to darken. Through the stars and mist, I watched Lia go sailing through the air till she smacked the wall of the hallway. She stayed suspended with her head pressed up against the ceiling, feet dangling in a panic. My purse and its contents were scattered across the floor.

With some unseen force, the Hunter kept me dangling in the air by my barely operable throat, but he turned and stepped toward Lia, pointing the blade at her.

"Phew, with a kick like that, it's a good thing this vessel doesn't need to procreate." He gently patted himself between the legs. His jovial air disappeared into a cruel, toothy grin. Perhaps, I should remove your potential for producing offspring. We certainly don't need any more of the Faithful running around!"

The tip of the knife began to singe Lia's shirt at the height of her bellybutton. Her breathing quickened, and she began to moan. I screamed in rage!

"You're here for me! Do your master's bidding and leave her alone!"

The knife flicked with a "ting" as it moved away from her stomach.

"You're right, of course. Business first." He stepped toward me but looked back at Lia over his shoulder and licked his lips. "Pleasure second."

He resumed his grip on my throat when he reached where

I had been dangling in the air. The orange left his eyes and Gamble's brown eyes looked deeply into mine. I thought for a moment that I caught a glimpse of the true man in there.

"I am sorry, Misty. It was either you or me."

He took a deep breath in through his nostrils as his eyes rolled back in his head. His right arm tensed as he prepared to strike.

"It is time for the advent of Sheol."

Gamble's brown eyes encircled black pupils that began to twist with bands of orange, and I could swear that his canine teeth began to grow in length while I was overcome with the anticipation of inescapable pain.

"I am the Blood Ward—"

My eyes went red and my face was suddenly hot and wet. My ears were ringing as I fell to the ground.

As soon as I hit the ground, I screamed wildly. I had no idea where I was. I kicked and backed myself all the way till I recognized the feeling of the door to my back porch. I finally processed that when I had been pushing myself back with my feet, I had kicked an unmoving leg. My scream continued at the feeling of what I believed to be somebody's corpse.

Arms arrested my squirming and after the ringing began to fade, a voice that I did not expect spoke soft and steady by my ear.

"Misty, Misty. It's going to be ok. Misty, it's over." The gentle touch rubbed and squeezed my shoulders. The voice that I at last recognized was Mark's!

I grabbed the hem of my shirt and wiped my face of what I already knew coated it. Looking up, I saw the quirky smile of Mark looking comfortingly at me. He looked terrified, but he was holding it together better than I was. We both heard Lia coughing. He backed away from me to go tend to her. When he rose and took a couple steps back, I saw my pistol held awkwardly in his hand. His grip on it told me that it was something he was unaccustomed to.

It was then that I looked down to my left and saw the lifeless body of Edward Gamble. I issued an irrepressible gasp when I saw that a portion of his head was removed, and human ichor was sprayed all over the wall next to me. That is an image that I can never unsee, nor a smell that I will ever forget.

I wish I grieved more for the man, but seeing the evil intent in his eyes, knowing the wicked things he had done... I feel no regret at his death. Perhaps that is not the godly approach. It will be hard to shake off this callousness.

What I share next is —I believe— of critical import for the trials that are surely yet to come. It is with a sense of dread that I bring them to words. Only moments after I gasped and Mark ensured that Lia was alright, the lights flickered then went out. A whirlwind of a roar blew through the house, accompanied by a dense black mist. The unlit house was dark, but the blackness that rode with the mist was distinctly different. It tore down the hallway, knocking us all to the ground again, and then the front door of the house exploded outward with a crack like a thunderbolt!

A few moments later, the roar had faded into the far night, and all the lights in the house began to flicker and then illuminate. Mark, Lia, and I all stared in stunned silence for several long moments.

Then, I looked to Lia and saw her bloody eyebrow and swollen lip and torn shirt. I thought of how much the girl had done to protect me. I was overcome. I crawled to her and embraced her. I cried into her shoulder and whispered in quiet affection.

"I can never repay you. I can never do enough. Oh, you dear girl. There is no other woman in the world like you!" I continued to cling to her and cry. She gently held my head and then began to cry herself.

Mark stepped back and dropped the gun where he found it next to my toppled purse.

At just that moment, I heard another voice calling out. This voice, however, I recognized instantly, and I cried aloud for Henry to come hold me!

He ran up and repeated my name countless times. He sputtered breathlessly, "Oh, I'm so sorry, baby. I'm so sorry!" He slumped down and pulled me into his lap. We wept together, and I melted into his embrace.

Grigory had rushed in with Henry and began tending to Lia in kind. His method of caring for her had a more medically geared approach, but after a few moments of nervous questioning and inspecting her injuries, their exchange resulted in a similarly tender resolution.

Marcus Spasmen's Personal Memoirs – (11:48 PM) July 11th, 2023

Two days since mom died. Two days since I proved again to be a terrible judge of character. Two days since I chased my former friend into the woods with the intent to kill him. Two days since I was nailed to the gate of Hell and was rebranded.

What led to the unraveling of the final strands in the Hunter's tapestry was not how he baited us into thinking that Chief Davidson was the final target. The Hunter described a leader whose fall would inevitably bring about the flames that "overcome". He also alluded to "the one who cast the last ballot". Fire Chief Davidson was on the city council, so he would be one to "cast ballots". This inference was strengthened, because he was the only surviving city council member. However, a chance glimpse tipped the scales of fate.

I went back to visit the library after all the necessary evidence was collected and the crime scene cleared. The last federal agent had climbed into an SUV that was backed into the corner of the parking lot. He sat in the black car and watched me intently behind a black windshield. How ironic that Misty's salvation and Gamble's damnation hinged upon a detail that was unobserved by all yet plainly displayed for anyone to see.

In fact, let me retrace my steps further. Best not to omit a detail!

First, I went to the cemetery, admittedly to curse the edifice of my disdain. However, I noticed that someone had already done it prior to my arrival, but their disdain was manifested in vandalism. The head of Christ had been broken off and replaced upside down. Pinned beneath the overturned cranium was the "Sixth Hunt".

Henry had just described the prior epistles to me, so I was eager to share this discovery with him. I immediately sent an image of the last installment in Gamble's twisted diaries to Henry. He interpreted the document and deduced, as was my first assumption, that Chief Davidson was the final target. Reportedly, he and Grig sped off like bats out of Hell to catch the killer. I made my way to the library, via the sidewalk, passing FBC Allison whilst texting Grig. I told him that I would join their convocation shortly, but there was one thing that I needed to do first.

I stood in the parking lot, surveying the road behind me, and beyond that the far wood line where the new construction sign foreboded an impending overhaul. I stood thunderstruck, at last connecting that the "vandals" mentioned in the letter were the council members who voted to clear the woods instead of leveling the library for the sake of a new factory to be built! The condemned piney realm housed the site of the crater, or what is better known as the Site of Dominion. Thus, the crux of Gamble's fixation was on the docket to be destroyed.

I thought our suspicions now totally confirmed at this revelation, so I then stepped inside, intentionally neglecting the CLOSED sign. The urge to go help Grig and Henry stirred within me, but a solemn duty to my mother's memory was owed. I needed closure. I needed to fully accept that she was gone. I walked into the silent building, looking about to see if anyone else was inside. No one was. Half of the lights in the main lobby were off, and the bookshelves that didn't get sprayed with blood and bile were moved further away from the spot where the ones that had formerly stood.

Anxiously, I made my way to the pillar where I once saw my mother, lifeless, rocking in my father's arms, suspended over a pool of her own bloody emesis. I stood there, at the spot, looking at the outdated checkered carpet and saw the checkers blanketed in a large circle of brownish red. I don't know how long I stared at that spot. Maybe a minute, maybe an hour. I just stared in morose silence, absorbing the confirmation that I needed. Mom was really gone.

Then in unfathomable horror, I looked ahead and saw dozens of dried pools of blood. My eyes watered and my throat caught, despite my best efforts to stay composed. So much loss. So much death.

To think how much I loved my mother, how her loss feels like someone cut away a chunk of my heart... that pain is duplicated to so many others on account of these two-dozen or so dried puddles! Fathers, mothers, sons, and daughters. All torn away... and for what? I trembled heavily and my vision blurred with pools of tears.

"WHY?!?" I screamed, voice echoing about the broad chamber.

After a few moments of sobbing in the dully lit room, with my hand leaning against the pillar, I heard the door open behind me.

"Son."

My father's voice made me stand up straighter. I tried to appear strong, but all the while, I still whimpered on the inside. After wiping my eyes, I turned around.

"Hey Dad."

His expression was so haggard. He finally looked his age. Somehow, despite working in the sun his whole life as a farmer, my dad never seemed to age. We joked that he was the youngest looking 65-year-old we'd ever known. Now, after Mom's passing, he appears to have lost his luster.

He smiled softly as he walked up to me. The closer he got, the weaker I became.

"Mark, why are you always alone?"

I wasn't sure what he meant by that question. I'm rather fond of solitude. I find it relaxing. I get this sense of freedom to do and be when I'm not waiting on someone else's schedule.

"Well, I'm not always alone. I have friends." My tears began to dry up as I became distracted by his question.

"I do admire the friends you have chosen, but I'm not talking about your friends. Why are *you* always alone?"

"Is this about me not having a girlfriend right now?" I asked, trying to navigate his question.

"Do you love me?"

His new question struck me like a punch in the gut.

"Pwa-what? Of course, I love you, Dad! I think the world of you and... you and mom. Why would you ask that?"

"It's just that we live so close by and I hardly ever see you."

My eyes watered at hearing my father's complaint. I looked to the dark stain on the ground and then back to him.

"Well, I promise that I'll be around more, Dad." I went to give him a hug. He squeezed me tight and then I heard something that I had never heard before. Dad began to cry. He pulled me tighter then he cried into my neck. At first, I was in disbelief, but that was quickly dispelled by the humble amazement that a man as tough as my father was broken, weeping on his son's shoulder. My own grief overcame me again, and I fervently hugged him back.

"What are you doing for supper tonight?" I asked, squeezing his shoulder after we finally pulled away from each other.

He wiped the tears that dripped from his white beard before responding.

"I don't know. I've been eating your momma's cooking for thirty-seven years. I'm not much good at anything besides burgers and breakfast food."

I smiled at him, "I like breakfast food."

He let out an exasperated laugh as a few more tears trickled from his eyes.

"I'm sorry dad, I'm going to be better about spending time with you. I promise."

The old farmer smiled and nodded his balding head.

It was in that moment, that a quick glimpse to the side of his nodding head, I saw the plaque, labeled "To the heroes who saved our library!"

My father must have noticed my eyes widen, because he nervously asked, "What is it, son? What's the matter?"

I didn't respond at first, I just kept staring in disbelief at what I failed to realize before! The city council was all there, in that picture, except for one member... Chief Billy Davidson. In his place stood Misty Loadwain. In fine print beneath the members listed was an annotation.

"Primary vote: October 2nd, 2022
Final vote: October 13th, 2022
With the debut of a fearless new leader in
the community, Misty Loadwain!"

The night of the final vote... Chief Davidson wasn't there.

I recall distinctly, October 13th was the day that Id tried to burn the foster home down. Davidson was at that fire. Misty had initially presented the vote, which was approved by Mayor Haldent.

My breath caught as the pieces clicked together in my mind. Misty was the "leader" mentioned in the Hunt. It wasn't Chief Billy Davidson who was the final target; it was Misty!

I instantly grabbed my phone and tried to call Henry and warn him as I ran out the door, paying no heed to my father's call. Henry never picked up the phone, so I sent him the picture that I already had taken of the plaque, then sent "MISTY IS THE LAST TARGET, NOT DAVIDSON!"

Not knowing whether Henry had received the information or not, I drove as fast as I could toward the Loadwain residence. I had just pulled into the driveway and opened the door of my car when I heard a scream from within and the sound of broken glass. Not knowing what I was even doing, I sprinted up the steps and ran into the house.

There he was... the Hunter, Edward Gamble, dressed in a grey robe, but emanating a shroud of black. The air was cold when I entered the hallway where he had Misty by the throat. Behind them, suspended in the air, pinned up against the wall was the flailing girlfriend of Grigory! At this point, I didn't even overreact to the bizarre supernatural things taking place, I kept my eyes fixed on Gamble. He didn't notice my approach. He was too busy talking to Misty while Lia kicked the wall repeatedly. My eyes caught the shape of a pistol on the ground, and without hesitation, I crept over to the weapon and picked it up. All that I heard was Gamble begin to say, "I am the—", but I had clenched my teeth in anticipation, so I heard nothing else until after my ears stopped ringing from the concussive shot.

Gamble fell instantly, and bits of his cerebrum were everywhere. It was horrifying. I couldn't stop shaking as I knelt and tried to console Misty, who was kicking and screaming in terror. She was veiled beneath a mask of Gamble's blood. She wiped her face, then calmed after I rubbed her shoulders for a few moments. I then went to check on Lia, who was beaten up, but appeared stable. Suddenly, a surge of shadow burst into the air, killing all the lights in the house as it departed from Gamble's corpse! It knocked us all over, then billowed down the hallway and —like a powder-keg— demolished the front door.

When everything quieted again and light had returned to the house, Misty crawled to Lia and embraced her, thanking her profusely. Their affectionate embrace filled me with solace. Genuine kindred love displayed was powerful enough to withdraw me from the dark dread that had fueled much of my actions the past few days.

Shortly following this tender moment, the thundering footsteps of Henry and Grigory entered the house. Each man assumed care of his woman and I stepped back. In disbelief, I looked at each of the ladies. They were safe. They were alive. I had done that. I had helped save somebody! Then I turned again to the motionless corpse with a gaping hole in its head... *but at what cost?*

I kept staring at the body. *I killed him. I killed that man.* He didn't look like a human anymore. His stillness and lack of color made him look like a mannequin. Did this mannequin really have an entire life story so complex, so full of experiences, passion, and purpose... just like mine? And I took that away? But his passion and purpose had succumbed to insanity. So, whether at the "demon's" behest, or Gamble's own lust for violence, his death was necessary. At least, that's what I'll have to tell myself to sleep at night. If there is such a thing as eternity, I sent him into it, and the gravity of that thought may haunt me forever.

I finally took my eyes off Gamble and looked on the two wonderful women who were still very much alive. They are safe. That is my consolation. I stepped away from the reunited couples and made my way to the remnants of the exploded door. A flurry of red and blue lights flashed off the surrounding trees as a cacophony of sirens cut short. The cavalry had arrived.

I knew that it would be a late supper, but I pulled out my phone and texted my dad anyway.

"Sorry that I had to run. It might be a late one, but are you still wanting to do breakfast for supper?"

In his usual inexpressive manner of texting, I received the solitary "thumbs up" symbol. I smiled as I tucked my phone back into my pocket, knowing that there was a mountain of love packed into that wordless icon.

The Third Prayer of Adam Clemmens –

(12:31 AM) July 12th, 2023

The hour of my greatest shame, the advent of my own soul's corruption came about like an unseen wave rising and crashing against the shore, obliterating the landscape.

I had finished constructing my barricade across the front driveway when I turned about just in time to spot Owen looking curiously over the fence into the neighbor's yard. The neighbor's boy hadn't been seen since Sunday morning before the chaff met for their church gathering. In fact, I hadn't seen any of the neighbors back since then.

"They got what they deserved." The whisper came.

What does that mean? They weren't among the number that were killed, were they?

He answered me in more whispers, as always.

Somewhere, deep down, my heart ached, even though they weren't chosen like I was to hear the true voice, the distant grief felt like the twisting of a knife within my gut.

Every thought of sorrow washed away as I saw Owen's head whip around looking at me. His guilty face gaped before he sprinted off back towards the house. He knew that he was being disobedient, and he knew that I was going to punish him for it. I watched him scramble up the trellis that led to the balcony over the pool patio. Before I knew what happened, I was dripping with rage. Beside myself, I stormed into the house.

Kelly must have been aware of what was going on, because when she saw my look of ire, she raised her hands pleading.

"The boy needs to learn to mind!" I said coldly.

Kelly's pleas became more assertive as she leaned against me to slow my approach toward Owen who now stood in the hallway to the stairs. Owen looked almost defiant in how he jutted his chin out toward me. The boy's resilience angered me even more.

I stomped over to the boy. He took a step back but did not run again. His mother pushed hard against my chest, yelling in protest. My eyes flashed red. Moments later when my sight returned, Kelly was on the ground, seeming to be unconscious. I had control of my actions, but the drive of every impulse was heightened to an all-consuming ecstasy. To meet my feelings of anger was an inundation of cathartic warmth. To scream and shout felt like the fears that I once held in were being scared off. To grip and squeeze felt like the perfect act of justice.

Owen gave a faint cry as I clamped down on his arm. His voice was somehow far off in my mind, as if echoing along a lengthy tunnel.

"You will learn to mind, boy." I spoke through gritted teeth, feeling a cold chill running up my spine.

Another voice was far down the tunnel too, but this time coming from the opposite end.

"Daddy, no! Daddy, please!"

Merrin's voice. It was so far away, and it sounded distorted. I wondered if she too had escaped the house and was calling from outside.

My red vision turned black. Flashing glimpses of Owen's pained expression as his arm was held in my clutches. These two sights alternated: a black, scaly wall and justice for a wrong done.

"Daddy, please stop! You're choking him!" I felt little hands thump against my back.

What does she mean that I'm choking him?

"Enough, child!" My voice now sounded distorted too. Something caused my skin to shiver. I lashed out with my free hand and flung Merrin across the room, landing next to her mother.

Seeing them both laying there, a pang of shame struck me. However, it was immediately swallowed up again by my rage. I whipped my head around, to face the boy who I had been restraining all the while. I saw the wall of black scales that enclosed me. I knew that I should be seeing my son there, but for some reason, my view was obscured. My hand still squeezed mercilessly in wrath.

Suddenly, the wall of black scales phased into a view of my hallway at home, and there stood Owen, his face purple and my hand latched around his neck!

I staggered for a moment, then the image distorted, and I saw my hand around Owen's arm again. He looked sad, but dutifully submissive to my grip. Confused, I spun my head around to look at Kelly. One moment, she quietly rocked back and forth on the ground, clutching her pregnant belly. The next moment, it was as if a different world was being shown to me. She sat there, contently waiting for me to finish reprimanding Owen so that she might take him and return him to his room. Then everything went black and I was behind a wall of pitch scales again.

I turned to where I knew Owen to be. The black wall remained for several moments, but then it phased to the glimpse of my son being strangled by my own hands again. I felt revulsion at the sight and I tried to pull away, but it felt as though another hand was squeezing my own around Owen's neck.

All too late, did I realize that I had been blinded and led so miserably astray! God had not been whispering to me all these days. I finally admitted that it had to be the Hunter!

In a panic, I looked to see what was happening to Merrin. Which phase of this torment was real for her? Was I strangling her too?

However, the sight of Merrin did not change when I looked at her. The image was crystal clear. She didn't phase between different postures of suffering. She just knelt there beside her mother, head bowed in my direction. Her eyes were closed, and her head was tilted forward.

I was strengthened by the sight of my resilient little girl, and at last, I raged against the darkness that held me there.

"Leave my family alone, Hunter!" My voice cracked in desperation.

The demon spoke back in a bated yet hushed tone.

"I... am... not... the Hunter."

My blood ran cold, and I felt like all was lost. Who could

withstand yet another spirit? The chilling voice continued.

"*I offer you a means of escaping your pain. I offer you a chance to right your wrongs, to undo your past mistakes. Trust in me. I will see that all your needs are met. You see, Adam, you can worship me and be free to live whatever life you like. All it takes is a little sacrifice.*"

My breathing became erratic. I wanted so badly to let go of Owen's throat, but this monster kept squeezing my hand.

"*I am he who demands your undying loyalty. I am Molech, and I will feed on the sacrifice of your children!*"

Tears began to pour from my face as I tried to wail aloud, but no sound escaped my mouth. I was trapped in a living nightmare, and my body had now committed to murdering my own children.

"Father."

The world seemed to shake as if lightning had struck the ground somewhere nearby. I saw what seemed to be gray streaks running through the black scaly walls in my mind.

"Father."

Her words had never cut me to the quick like this before. Something powerful rode on her call. The oppressive night in my vision began to fail as glints of light started to pierce between the scales. The shakiness of my sight began to lessen.

The tensile voice in my head then whispered in haste, with palpable dread,

"*Quick, kill the girl! Then your sacrifice will be accepted, and I will give you al—*"

His words abruptly changed to a fleeing screech when Merrin cried once again,

"Father!"

Light shot clear through the scales in my mind, then everything exploded apart, giving way to a brilliant world of white and unending beauty and fresh air, as if it were the first breath I'd taken in ages.

Although that glorious vision was something new to my sight, my soul felt a familiar sense of rest. Only for a moment, I beheld the River of Life, and I knew that what had been plaguing my house was no longer there. After a time, my vision of the bright, lush expanse faded, and I returned with teary eyes to my house.

Owen was huddled up, terrified. He had finger shaped bruises on his neck.

I cried aloud in agony and then crumpled before my son, weeping and apologizing profusely. He sniffled and his lip quivered as he cautiously approached me. His mistrust broke my heart, but I couldn't blame him. I had nearly killed him.

I turned to Merrin and Kelly who were huddling together and weeping.

I knelt in the midst of my family sprawled across the floor of our hallway.

"Oh God, please forgive me. Please, please forgive me!" I wailed.

I was consumed with sorrow. I know now that my family had been oppressed by another demon. Despite my failures, I am still one of God's children, and so it makes sense that this demon had no power to possess me, but he masterfully distorted my sight.

I isolated myself and my family from the church. In the isolation, this demon whispered in my ear, causing me to think that I was somehow special and deserving of uncommon revelation. My fear was his fuel. I took my eyes off Christ and my self-absorbed vision was accompanied by a servant of the devil.

Inches from killing my family, I fell subject to his devices, nearly doing what Id failed to accomplish last autumn. But the faith of a child saved us! Merrin called aloud, "Father", but she was not calling to me. She cried to Abba, the Everlasting Father, and He saved us!

Oh God, thank You for this salvation! I promise to keep my eyes on You. I promise to come to know Your voice better. Please give me faith to pursue You the right way and to hold my precious family close to You.

EPILOGUE
<u>Henry Paul Loadwain's Journal – (2140) 18 July 2023</u>

It's funny how quickly your whole mindset can shift at a word. One hour, I'm convinced beyond any doubt that Davidson's life was in jeopardy, and I was committed with all my being to stop the Hunter before he killed again. Then after a text message from Mark, my universe shifted, and I found myself speeding back across town before my brain could catch up.

Before that, however, Grigory and I had made it to Chief Davidson's house. I knocked on the door of the impressive log cabin that was tucked in the back corner of Bear Paw Creek. The cabin looked as though the entire neighborhood had sprung up around it. All other homes further up the road were newer constructions with cookie cutter designs of lofted ceilings, broad windows permitting easy views into the entryways of the houses. Those wide windows bragged of chandeliers and elegant staircases. Chief Davidson's house was much older. It was the embodiment of Allison's rustic origins. Simple, strong, enduring.

My knuckle rapped against the dense wooden door. The sound was dull, because the entrance was crafted of solid lumber and not cheap composite materials. I thought no one would hear me at first because of the suppressed tone. However, just before I used the meat of my palm to thump loudly, the curtain to the left of the door shifted and I saw Davidson's face and another beside his peering out at me. Staring blatantly at the men, I gestured for them to open the door.

The latch loosed and the heavy door opened.

"Come on in, boys. Geez, Grig, are you a cop now? What are

you even doing here? I thought I said that all off-duty personnel needed to remain at home until the Hunter was captured."

Grig tipped his head forward in a sign of respect.

"Yes sir, you did."

"Then why are you here at my house?"

I chimed in to Grig's defense.

"Sir, we have reason to believe that you are the Hunter's next target."

At this, Captain Andrews drew a pistol from his waist and spun about the room. He frantically aimed in every direction.

"Woah, woah, woah" I said, raising my arms to settle him.

Andrews began checking hall closets and then finally relocked the door behind us.

"Larry, would you chill out? What's he gonna do, take on the four of us?"

Grig and I exchanged glances, knowing full well the probability of that. We once had an all-out brawl with the possessed man, Lionel, and we no longer carry much confidence in the strength of men.

"Sir, there's more."

Andrews came back to our circle and finally holstered his pistol. Davidson tilted his head forward and raised an eyebrow, indicating that he was ready to listen.

"The Hunter is Edward Gamble."

"Damn, that's not good. The killer has tactical training and knows intimately how your department operates."

I went ahead and winced, knowing that he wasn't going to believe what more I had to say.

"Aaand he's possessed by a demon."

"Oh, here we go!" Andrews interjected, throwing his hands in the air.

I turned sharply toward my left side where he stood. I was taken aback by his response. I remember reading Grigory's journal of the night that Andrews was attacked by Id in the foster home fire. Andrews had encountered a demon first-hand, but now he's acting as if I'm just saying a bunch of hogwash.

"Henry..." Davidson spoke hesitantly. "I'm a God-fearing man, just like you..." He paused, thinking about what he was going to say next. "But all this talk of demons and angels and supernatural events happening in Allison. It just... eh... it doesn't happen anywhere else. You see, the rest of the time. In all of my career, and yours, there's an explanation that can be rationalized out by human means. I'm not saying that God don't exist, nor am I denying the existence of demons or the devil, but is this really that?"

I tried to take a moment or two and collect myself. Grig and I have been through so much spiritual warfare at this point, that demonic influence was as obvious as the moon in the night sky.

"Chief—"

"Oh, come on now, Henry!" Andrews interrupted belligerently.

"Captain Andrews," Grig piped up. "I know it sounds crazy, but remember when we were in the foster home fire and you were trapped in that side room? Don't you remember being attacked by that demon?"

Andrews shook his head violently. "I don't know what you're talking about, boy. You've gotten way too involved in all this occult nonsense. You're a firefighter, not a detective. Stay in your lane, young man."

Andrews turned to me and spoke in an only slightly more tamed voice, "Henry, I know we've had our differences in the past, but Gamble is just a man. A sick, twisted man."

"Regardless, gentlemen..." Chief Davidson spoke over Andrews. "You're saying that you have evidence that points toward me being the next target for the Hunter? What evidence have you got?"

"Each of the kills that Gamble has made, except for Jenny and the congregation of FBC Allison, have been city council members. You are now the only surviving member. The only reason he killed Jenny was because she suspected him and got too close. And the massacre at FBC Allison was intended to kill as many Christians as possible, yes, but his primary target was

Pastor Kent. We have found that all the kills have been tied to short letters in which a hunter describes killing prey. Each murder has a correlating narrative."

I reached for my phone to show him the picture of the Sixth Hunt so that he could read it himself. I continued explaining while fishing it out of my pocket.

"Today, a new letter has been found, but no one else has been killed yet. The way he describes his target, it all points to y—."

Grig told me later that I suddenly stopped speaking as I looked down at my phone screen. I had missed a call from Mark, and a text message that read:

"MISTY IS THE LAST TARGET, NOT DAVIDSON!"

I stared in anxious confusion for a long moment at those words, then opened my phone so I could see a full-sized picture of a plaque, with Misty standing amongst a group of people: Kent, Simm, Haldent, and Knox. Davidson wasn't in that picture. Grigory leaned over my shoulder to inspect the text and picture as well.

My heart started to pound out of my chest. I paid little attention at that time to a strange remark made by Andrews when I looked up from the picture. He had turned to the fire chief, grabbed his shoulder and said, "Don't worry, Chief. I won't let Gamble take you down." Then he slowly added, "Trust in me. I will see that all your needs are met."

(I'm noting here as a reminder for Tommy and me to have another conversation with Andrews. Considering recent events, I've generated many more questions for him. I've got to figure out what he and Carlyle were doing at the Mayor's mansion that night!)

At the time, I dismissed Andrew's promises as bravado while zooming in to the picture on my phone. Unaware of recent events reported to me by Adam, I kept my focus on the dates of the plaque, and at last, Mark's message made sense.

"Misty!" I half-whispered in terror as I spun round, unlatched the door and sprinted to the car. I nearly left Grig behind, but thankfully he was quick on the uptake and he vaulted down the steps of the log-cabin porch and jumped into the car. The rest of the trip home was a blur while my vision fuzzed and my temples throbbed. We arrived on muscle memory and adrenaline.

✝

To see Mark standing there, over Gamble's body, knowing that he killed for Misty's sake when I wasn't there to protect her, it... it's staggering. She was vulnerable, and I was nowhere nearby. If not for Mark... It takes my breath away to think about it. I'm indebted to my friend forever, and I will never stop saying "thank you".

✝

It's now been a week since Misty and Lia were attacked. Misty is finally well enough to have visitors, so after discussing it with her, she agreed to invite the newly engaged Grigory and Lia over for a steak dinner! And of course, we bought the biggest steak for our guest of honor, Mark.

Something has changed in that man. I'm not quite sure what's different, but there's an air of growing peace within him. He doesn't seem as lost or conflicted as he once did. I don't know how that makes any sense, though. If you think of all that he's been through, he should be living in a catatonic state. Honestly, I think it's clear that God's grace is preserving him for something greater.

There are some details that I feel like we have no way of learning more about now, since the Hunter is gone. Both Mark and Misty described a dark, roaring fog that blasted through the house. My missing front door is evidence of that. Their description leaves me to believe that the demon that we know as the Hunter has left Allison for now. His current plan failed. His vessel... slain.

However, I can only begin to imagine what Gamble meant when he described a beast who awaits awakening and whose fill will be humanity. And I'm assuming that the Hunter wanted to perform the rites of dominion, like Id. Evidently not for himself, but for his "Master", as if the completion of the rites would have ushered in the Devil to come rule the earth. It seems... If Gamble hadn't been stopped, not only would I have lost my wife and Grig his fiancé, but biblical tribulation would have begun!

Were we even supposed to try and keep Revelation from happening? Surely, it wasn't supposed to come about like that, but I can't imagine that the Hunter is simply done with us after losing one vessel. And what are we to do with the information Adam just gave me? Is there really another demon haunting us alongside the Hunter? Could it really be the Molech of the Old Testament?

How? How can we survive this?

Banishing those anxious thoughts, I stood against my back door, with tray of seasoned, raw steaks in my hand, ready to go on the grill, and I watched while growing a smile on my face. Lia and Misty were sitting on the couch, excitedly talking about wedding plans, while Grig and Mark stood in the hall, comparing their favorite running shoes. The air was lively, for the first time in a long time. I clicked the tongs to satisfaction and opened the back door to the porch.

I took a deep breath with my eyes closed, allowing them to adjust to the setting light that always beams right in my face when I step outside at 1800. I eagerly anticipated listening to the babbling brook in concert with steaks sizzling on the grill. I heard the brook, but instead of smelling flowers or freshly cut grass, I detected a heavy, metallic odor. I opened my eyes as the porch door shut behind me.

The beam of light lessened in its intensity as I looked down at the wooden planks of the porch.

I dropped the entire tray of steaks without a second thought. The sound must have alarmed Grigory and Mark, because they both rushed out the door behind me and stopped, each on either of my shoulders. After their eyes adjusted to the light, I heard Mark exclaim,

"My God..."

"Oh no..." Grigory breathed out.

I took a step back and held my breath for what felt like an eternity as I looked and saw a giant bloody "V" painted over much of my porch. Its point was aimed directly at my house.

LEVI ARMSTRONG

After finally taking a breath, I spoke in a listless whisper. "This is the Rite of Choosing."

192